Frank Richard Stockton

The Shadrach

And other Stories

Frank Richard Stockton

The Shadrach
And other Stories

ISBN/EAN: 9783743367494

Manufactured in Europe, USA, Canada, Australia, Japa

Cover: Foto ©Andreas Hilbeck / pixelio.de

Manufactured and distributed by brebook publishing software (www.brebook.com)

Frank Richard Stockton

The Shadrach

THE SHADRACH

AND OTHER STORIES

BY

FRANK R STOCKTON

.

LONDON

W H ALLEN & CO LIMITED

13 WATERLOO PLACE SW

1893

CONTENTS.

THE SHADRACH 1

ASAPH 41

MY TERMINAL MORAINE 107

THE PHILOSOPHY OF RELATIVE EXISTENCES ... 177

THE KNIFE THAT KILLED PO HANCY ... 190

THE REV. EZEKIEL CRUMP 222

GRANDISON'S QUANDARY 255

THE SHADRACH

AND OTHER STORIES.

THE SHADRACH.

WHENEVER I make a Christmas present I
like it to mean something, not necessarily
my sentiments toward the person to whom I give
it, but sometimes an expression of what I should
like that person to do or to be.   In the early part
of a certain winter not very long ago, I found myself in a position of perplexity and anxious con-
cern regarding a Christmas present which I wished
to make.

The state of the case was this.   There was a
young lady, the daughter of a neighbour and old
friend of my father, who had been gradually as-

suming relations towards me which were not only unsatisfactory to me, but were becoming more and more so. Her name was Mildred Bronce. She was between twenty and twenty-five years of age, and as fine a woman in every way as one would be likely to meet in a lifetime. She was handsome, of a tender and generous disposition, a fine intelligence, and a thoroughly well-stocked mind. We had known each other for a long time, and when fourteen or fifteen, Mildred had been my favourite companion. She was a little younger than I, and I liked her better than any boy I knew. Our friendship had continued through the years, but of late there had been a change in it; Mildred had become very fond of me, and her fondness seemed to have in it certain elements which annoyed me.

As a girl to make love to no one could be better than Mildred Bronce; but I never made love to her—at least not earnestly—and I did not wish that any permanent condition of loving should be established between us. Mildred did not seem to share this opinion, for every day it became plainer to me that she looked upon me as a lover, and that she was perfectly willing to return my affection.

But I had other ideas upon the subject. Into the rural town in which my family passed the greater part of the year there had recently come a young lady, Miss Janet Clinton, to whom my soul went out of my own option. In some respects, perhaps, she was not the equal of Mildred, but she was very pretty, she was small, she had a lovely mouth, was apparently of a clinging nature, and her dark eyes looked into mine with a tingling effect that no other eyes had ever produced. I was in love with her because I wished to be, and the consciousness of this fact caused me a proud satisfaction. This affair was not the result of circumstances, but of my own free will.

I wished to retain Mildred's friendship, I wished to make her happy ; and with this latter intent in view I wished very much that she should not disappoint herself in her anticipations of the future.

Each year it had been my habit to make Mildred a Christmas present, and I was now looking for something to give her which would please her and suit my purpose.

When a man wishes to select a present for a lady which, while it assures her of his kind feeling toward her, will at the same time indicate that not only has he no matrimonial inclinations in her direction, but that it would be entirely unwise for her to have any such inclinations in his direction; that no matter with what degree of fondness her heart is disposed to turn toward him, his heart does not turn toward her, and that, in spite of all sentiments induced by long association and the natural fitness of things, she need never expect to be to him anything more than a sister, he has, indeed, a difficult task before him. But such was the task which I set for myself.

Day after day I wandered through the shops. I looked at odd pieces of jewellry and bric-à-brac, and at many a quaint relic or bit of art work which seemed to have a meaning; but nothing had the meaning I wanted. As to books, I found none which satisfied me; not one which was adapted to produce the exact impression that I desired.

One afternoon I was in a little basement shop kept by a fellow in a long overcoat, who, so far as I was able to judge, bought curiosities but never sold any. For some minutes I had been looking

at a beautifully decorated saucer of rare workman-
ship for which there was no cup to match, and for
which the proprietor informed me no cup could
now be found or manufactured. There were some
points in the significance of an article of this sort,
given as a present to a lady, which fitted to my
purpose, but it would signify too much : I did not
wish to suggest to Mildred that she need never expect to find a cup. It would be better, in fact, if I
gave her anything of this kind, to send her a cup
and saucer entirely unsuited to each other, and
which could not, under any conditions, be used
together.

I put down the saucer, and continued my search
among the dusty shelves and cases.

"How would you like a paper-weight ?" the
shopkeeper asked. "Here is something a little
odd," handing me a piece of dark-coloured mineral
nearly as big as my fist, flat on the underside and
of a pleasing irregularity above. Around the
bottom was a band of arabesque work in some
dingy metal, probably German silver. I smiled as
I took it.

"This is not good enough for a Christmas

present," I said. "I want something odd, but it must have some value."

"Well," said the man, "that has no real value, but there is a peculiarity about it which interested me when I heard of it, and so I bought it. This mineral is a piece of what the iron-workers call shadrach. It is a portion of the iron or iron ore which passes through the smelting-furnaces without being affected by the great heat, and so they have given it the name of one of the Hebrew youths who was cast into the fiery furnace by Nebuchadnezzar, and who came out unhurt. Some people think there is a sort of magical quality about this shadrach, and that it can give out to human beings something of its power to keep their minds cool when they are in danger of being overheated. The old gentleman who had this made was subject to fits of anger, and he thought this piece of shadrach helped to keep him from giving way to them. Occasionally he used to leave it in the house of a hot-tempered neighbour, believing that the testy individual would be cooled down for a time, without knowing how the change had been brought about. I bought a lot of things of the old gentleman's widow, and this among them. I thought I might try it some time, but I never have."

I held the shadrach in my hand, ideas concerning it rapidly flitting through my mind. Why would not this be a capital thing to give to Mildred? If it should, indeed, possess the quality ascribed to it; if it should be able to cool her liking for me, what better present could I give her? I did not hesitate long.

" I will buy this," I said ; " but the ornamentation must be of a better sort. It is now too cheap and tawdry-looking."

" I can attend to that for you," said the shop-keeper. " I can have it set in a band of gold or silver filigree-work like this, if you choose."

I agreed to this proposition, but ordered the band to be made of silver, the cool tone of that metal being more appropriate to the characteristics of the gift than the warmer hues of gold.

When I gave my Christmas present to Mildred she was pleased with it; its oddity struck her fancy.

" I don't believe anybody ever had such a paper-weight as that," she said, as she thanked me. " What is it made of ? "

I told her, and explained what shadrach was ; but I did not speak of its presumed influence over human beings, which, after all, might be nothing but the wildest fancy. I did not feel altogether at my ease, as I added that it was merely a trifle, a thing of no value, except as a reminder of the season.

" The fact that it is a present from you gives it value," she said, as she smilingly raised her eyes to mine.

I left her house—we were all living in the city then—with a troubled conscience. What a deception I was practising upon this noble girl, who, if she did not already love me, was plainly on the point of doing so. She had received my present as if it indicated a warmth of feeling on my part, when, in fact, it was the result of a desire for a cooler feeling on her part.

But I called my reason to my aid, and I showed myself that what I had given Mildred—if it should prove to possess any virtue at all—was, indeed, a most valuable boon. It was something which would prevent the waste of her affections, the wreck of her hopes. No kindness could be truer, no regard for her happiness more sincere, than the motives which prompted me to give her the shadrach.

I did not soon again see Mildred, but now as often as possible I visited Janet. She always received me with a charming cordiality, and if this should develop into warmer sentiments I was not the man to wish to cool them. In many ways Janet seemed much better suited to me than Mildred. One of the greatest charms of this beautiful girl was a tender trustfulness, as if I were a being on whom she could lean and to whom she could look up. I liked this; it is very different from Mildred's manner; with the latter I had always been well satisfied if I felt myself standing on the same plane.

The weeks and months passed on, and again we were all in the country; and here I saw Mildred often. Our homes were not far apart, and our families were very intimate. With my opportunities for frequent observation, I could not doubt that a change had come over her. She was always

friendly when we met, and seemed as glad to see
me as she was to see any other member of my
family, but she was not the Mildred I used to
know.   It was plain that my existence did not
make the impression on her that it once made.
She did not seem to consider it important whether
I came or went; whether I was in the room or
not; whether I joined a party or stayed away. All
this had been very different.   I knew well that
Mildred had been used to consider my presence
as a matter of much importance, and I now felt
sure that my Christmas shadrach was doing its
work.   Mildred was cooling toward me.   Her
affection, or, to put it more modestly, her tendency
to affection, was gently congealing into friendship.
This was highly gratifying to my moral nature, for
every day I was doing my best to warm the soul of
Janet.   Whether or not I succeeded in this I could
not be sure.   Janet was as tender and trustful and
charming as ever, but no more so than she had
been months before.

Sometimes I thought she was waiting for an
indication of an increased warmth of feeling on my
part before she allowed the temperature of her

own sentiments to rise. But for one reason and another I delayed the solution of this problem. Janet was very fond of company, and although we saw a great deal of each other, we were not often alone. If we two had more frequently walked, driven, or rowed together, as Mildred and I used to do, I think Miss Clinton would soon have had every opportunity of making up her mind about the fervour of my passion.

The summer weeks passed on, and there was no change in the things which now principally concerned me, except that Mildred seemed to be growing more and more indifferent to me. From having seemed to care no more for me than for her other friends, she now seemed to care less for me than for most people. I do not mean that she showed a dislike, but she treated me with a sort of indifference which I did not fancy at all. This sort of thing had gone too far, and there was no knowing how much further it would go. It was plain enough that the shadrach was overdoing the business.

I was now in a state of much mental disquietude. Greatly as I desired to win the love of Janet, it grieved me to think of losing the generous friendship of Mildred—that friendship to which I had been accustomed for the greater part of my life, and on which, as I now discovered, I had grown to depend.

In this state of mind I went to see Mildred. I found her in the library writing. She received me pleasantly, and was sorry her father was not at home, and begged that I would excuse her finishing the note on which she was engaged, because she wished to get it into the post-office before the mail closed. I sat down on the other side of the table, and she finished her note, after which she went out to give it to a servant.

Glancing about me, I saw the shadrach. It was partly under a litter of papers, instead of lying on them. I took it up, and was looking at it when Mildred returned. She sat down and asked me if I had heard of the changes that were to be made in the time-table of the railroad. We talked a little on the subject, and then I spoke of the shadrach, saying carelessly that it might be interesting to analyse the bit of metal; there was a little knob which might be filed off without injuring it in the least.

"You may take it," she said, "and make what experiments you please. I do not use it much ; it is unnecessarily heavy for a paper-weight."

From her tone I might have supposed that she had forgotten that I had given it to her. I told her that I would be very glad to borrow the paper-weight for a time, and, putting it into my pocket, I went away, leaving her arranging her disordered papers on the table, and giving quite as much regard to this occupation as she had given to my little visit.

I could not feel sure that the absence of the shadrach would cause any diminution in the coolness of her feelings toward me, but there was reason to believe that it would prevent them from growing cooler. If she should keep that shadrach she might in time grow to hate me. I was very glad that I had taken it from her.

My mind easier on this subject, my heart turned more freely toward Janet, and, going to her house the next day I was delighted to find her alone. She was as lovely as ever, and as cordial, but she was flushed and evidently annoyed.

" I am in a bad humour to-day," she said, "and I

am glad you came to talk to me and quiet me. Dr. Gilbert promised to take me to drive this afternoon, and we were going over to the hills where they find the wild rhododendron. I am told that it is still in blossom up there, and I want some flowers ever so much—I am going to paint them. And besides, I am crazy to drive with his new horses ; and now he sends me a note to say he is engaged."

This communication shocked me, and I began to talk to her about Dr. Gilbert. I soon found that several times she had been driving with this handsome young physician, but never, she said, behind his new horses, nor to the rhododendron hills.

Dr. Hector Gilbert was a fine young fellow, beginning practice in town, and one of my favourite associates. I had never thought of him in connection with Janet, but I could now see that he might make a most dangerous rival. When a young and talented doctor, enthusiastic in his studies, and earnestly desirous of establishing a practice, and who, if his time were not fully occupied, would naturally wish that the neighbours would think that such were the case, deliberately devotes some hours on I know not how many sunny days to driving a young lady into the surrounding country, it may be supposed that he is really in love with her. Moreover, judging from Janet's present mood, this doctor's attentions were not without encouragement.

I went home; I considered the state of affairs; I ran my fingers through my hair; I gazed steadfastly upon the floor. Suddenly I rose. I had an inspiration; I would give the shadrach to Dr. Gilbert.

I went immediately to the doctor's office, and found him there. He was not in a very good humour.

"I have had two old ladies here nearly all the afternoon, and they have bored me to death," he said. "I could not get rid of them, because I found they had made an appointment with each other to visit me to-day and talk over a hospital plan which I proposed some time ago, and which is really very important to me, but I wish they had chosen some other time to come here. What is that thing?"

"That is a bit of shadrach," I said, "made into a paper-weight." And then I proceeded to explain what shadrach is, and what peculiar properties it must possess to resist the power of heat, which melts other metals apparently of the same class ; and I added that I thought it might be interesting to analyse a bit of it and discover what fire-proof constituents it possessed.

" I should like to do that," said the doctor, attentively turning over the shadrach in his hand. " Can I take off a piece of it?"

" I will give it to you," said I, "and you can make what use of it you please. If you do analyse it, I shall be very glad indeed to hear the results of your investigations."

The doctor demurred a little at taking the paper-weight with such a pretty silver ring around it, but I assured him that the cost of the whole affair was trifling, and I should be gratified if he would take it. He accepted the gift, and was thanking me, when a patient arrived, and I departed.

I really had no right to give away this paper-weight, which, in fact, belonged to Mildred, but there are times when a man must keep his eyes on the chief good, and not think too much about other things. Besides, it was evident that Mildred did not care in the least for the bit of metal, and she had virtually given it to me.

There was another point which I took into consideration. It might be that the shadrach might simply cool Dr. Gilbert's feelings toward me, and that would be neither pleasant nor advantageous. If I could have managed matters so that Janet could have given it to him, it would have been all right. But now all that I could do was to wait and see what would happen. If only the thing would cool the doctor in a general way, that would help. He might then give more thought to his practice and his hospital ladies, and let other people take Janet driving.

About a week after this I met the doctor; he seemed in a hurry, but I stopped him. I had a curiosity to know if he had analysed the shadrach, and asked him about it.

"No," said he; "I haven't done it. I haven't had time. I knocked off a piece of it, and I will attend to it when I get a chance. Good-day."

Of course if the man was busy he could not be expected to give his mind to a trifling matter of

C

that sort, but I thought that he need not have been so curt about it. I stood gazing after him as he walked rapidly down the street. Before I resumed my walk I saw him enter the Clinton house. Things were not going on well. The shadrach had not cooled Dr. Gilbert's feelings toward Janet.

But because the doctor was still warm in his attentions to the girl I loved, I would not in the least relax my attentions to her. I visited her as often as I could find an excuse to do so. There was generally someone else there, but Janet's disposition was of such gracious expansiveness that each one felt obliged to be satisfied with what he got, much as he may have wished for something different.

But one morning Janet surprised me. I met her at Mildred's house, where I had gone to borrow a book of reference. Although I had urged her not to put herself to so much trouble, Mildred was standing on a little ladder looking for the book, because, she said, she knew exactly what I wanted, and she was sure she could find the proper volume better than I could. Janet had been sitting in a window-seat reading, but when I came in she put down her book and devoted herself to conversation with me. I was a little sorry for this, because Mildred was very kindly engaged in doing me a service, and I really wanted to talk to her about the book she was looking for. Mildred showed so much of her old manner this morning that I would have been very sorry to have her think that I did not appreciate her returning interest in me. Therefore, while under other circumstances I would have been delighted to talk to Janet, I did not wish to give her so much of my attention then. But Janet Clinton was a girl who insisted on people attending to her when she wished them to do so, and having stepped through an open door into the garden, she presently called me to her. Of course I had to go.

"I will not keep you a minute from your fellow-student," she said, "but I want to ask a favour of you." And into her dark, uplifted eyes there came a look of tender trustfulness clearer than any I had yet seen there. "Don't *you* want to drive me to the rhododendron hills?" she said. "I suppose the flowers are all gone by this time, but I have never been there, and I should like ever so much to go."

I could not help remarking that I thought Dr. Gilbert was going to take her there.

"Dr. Gilbert, indeed!" she said with a little laugh. "He promised once, and didn't come, and the next day he planned for it it rained. I don't think doctors make very good escorts, anyway, for you can't tell who is going to be sick just as you are about to start on a trip. Besides, there is no knowing how much botany I should have to hear, and when I go on a pleasure-drive I don't care very much about studying things. But of course I don't want to trouble you."

"Trouble!" I exclaimed. "It will give me the greatest delight to take you that drive or any other, and at whatever time you please."

"You are always so good and kind," she said, with her dark eyes again upraised. "And now let us go in and see if Mildred has found the book."

I spoke the truth when I said that Janet's proposition delighted me. To take a long drive with that charming girl, and at the same time to feel that she had chosen me as her companion, was a greater joy than I had yet had reason to expect; but it would have been a more satisfying joy if she had

asked me in her own house and not in Mildred's;
if she had not allowed the love which I hoped was
growing up between her and me to interfere with
the revival of the old friendship between Mildred
and me.

But when we returned to the library Mildred was
sitting at a table with a book before her, opened at
the passage I wanted.

"I have just found it," she said with a smile.
"Draw up a chair, and we will look over these
maps together. I want you to show me how he
travelled when he left his ship."

"Well, if you two are going to the pole," said
Janet, with her prettiest smile, "I will go back to
my novel."

She did not seem in the least to object to my
geographical researches with Mildred, and if the
latter had even noticed my willingness to desert
her at the call of Janet, she did not show it. Apparently she was as much a good comrade as she
had ever been. This state of things was gratifying
in the highest degree. If I could be loved by Janet
and still keep Mildred as my friend, what greater
earthly joys could I ask?

The drive with Janet was postponed by wet weather. Day after day it rained, or the skies were heavy, and we both agreed that it must be in the bright sunshine that we would make this excursion. When we should make it, and should be alone together on the rhododendron hill, I intended to open my soul to Janet.

It may seem strange to others, and at the time it also seemed strange to me, but there was another reason besides the rainy weather which prevented my declaration of love to Janet. This was a certain nervous anxiety in regard to my friendship for Mildred. I did not in the least waver in my intention to use the best endeavours to make the one my wife, but at the same time I was oppressed by a certain alarm that in carrying out this project I might act in such a way as to wound the feelings of the other.

This disposition to consider the feelings of Mildred became so strong that I began to think that my own sentiments were in need of control. It was not right that while making love to one woman I should give so much consideration to my relations with another. The idea struck me that in a measure I had shared the fate of those who had thrown the Hebrew youths into the fiery furnace. My heart had not been consumed by the flames, but in throwing the shadrach into what I supposed were Mildred's affections, it was quite possible that I had been singed by them. At any rate my conscience told me that under the circumstances my sentiments toward Mildred were too warm; in honestly making love to Janet I ought to forget them entirely.

It might have been a good thing, I told myself, if I had not given away the shadrach, but kept it as a gift from Mildred. Very soon after I reached this conclusion it became evident to me that Mildred was again cooling in my direction as rapidly as the mercury falls after sunset on a September day. This discovery did not make my mercury fall ; in fact, it brought it for a time nearly to the boiling point. I could not imagine what had happened. I almost neglected Janet, so anxious was I to know what had made this change in Mildred.

Weeks passed on, and I discovered nothing except that Mildred had now become more than indifferent to me. She allowed me to see that my companionship did not give her pleasure.

Janet had her drive to the rhododendron hills, but she took it with Dr. Gilbert, and not with me. When I heard of this it pained me, though I could not help admitting that I deserved the punishment; but my surprise was almost as great as my pain, for Janet had recently given me reason to believe that she had a very small opinion of the young doctor. In fact, she had criticised him so severely that I had been obliged to speak in his defence. I now found myself in a most doleful quandary, and there was only one thing of which I could be certain—I needed cooling toward Mildred if I still allowed myself to hope to marry Janet.

One afternoon I was talking to Mr. Bronce in his library, when, glancing towards the table used by his daughter for writing purposes, I was astounded to see, lying on a little pile of letters, the Christmas shadrach. As soon as I could get an opportunity I took it in my hand and eagerly examined it. I had not been mistaken. It was the paper-weight I had given Mildred,

There was the silver band around it, and there was the place where a little piece had been knocked off by the doctor. Mildred was not at home, but I determined that I would wait and see her. I would dine with the Bronces; I would spend the evening ; I would stay all night ; I would not leave the house until I had had this mystery explained. She returned in about half an hour, and greeted me in the somewhat stiff manner she had adopted of late ; but when she noticed my perturbed expression and saw that I held the shadrach in my hand, she took a seat by the table, where for some time I had been waiting for her, alone.

"I suppose you want to ask me about that paper-weight ? "

"Indeed I do," I replied. "How in the world did you happen to get it again ? "

"Again ? " she repeated, satirically. "You may well say that. I will explain it to you. Some little time ago I called on Janet Clinton, and on her writing-desk I saw that paper-weight. I remembered it perfectly. It was the one you gave me last Christmas, and afterward borrowed of me, saying that you wanted to analyse it, or something of the sort. I had never used it very much, and of course was willing that you should take it, and make experiments with it if you wanted to ; but I must say that the sight of it on Janet Clinton's desk both shocked and angered me. I asked her where she had got it, and she told me a gentleman had given it to her. I did not waste any words in inquiring who this gentleman was, but I determined that she should not rest under a mistake in regard to its proper owner-ship, and told her plainly that the person who had given it to her had previously given it to me ; that it was mine, and he had no right to give it to anyone else. 'Oh, if that is the case,' she exclaimed, 'take it, I beg of you. I don't care for it, and what is more, I don't care any more for the man who gave it to me than I do for the thing itself.' So I took it and brought it home with me. Now you know how I happen to have it again."

For a moment I made no answer. Then I asked her how long it had been since she had received the shadrach from Janet Clinton.

"Oh, I don't remember exactly," she said; "it was several weeks ago."

Now I knew everything; all the mysteries of the past were revealed to me. The young doctor, fervid in his desire to please the woman he loved, had given Janet this novel paper-weight. From that moment she had begun to regard his attentions with apathy, and finally—her nature was one which was apt to go to extremes—to dislike him. Mildred repossessed herself of the shadrach which she took, not as a gift from Janet, but as her rightful property, presented to her by me. And this horrid little object, probably with renewed power, had cooled, almost frozen, indeed, the sentiments of that dear girl toward me. Then, too, had the spell been taken from Janet's inclinations, and she had gone to the rhododendron hills with Doctor Gilbert.

One thing was certain. *I* must have that shadrach.

"Mildred," I exclaimed, "will you not give me this paper-weight? Give it to me for my own?"

"What do you want to do with it?" she asked sarcastically. "Analyse it again?"

"Mildred," said I, "I did not give it to Janet. I gave it to Dr. Gilbert, and he must have given it to her. I know I had no right to give it away at all, but I did not believe that you would care ; but now I beg that you will let me have it. Let me have it for my own. I assure you solemnly I will never give it away. It has caused trouble enough already."

"I don't exactly understand what you mean by trouble," she said, "but take it if you want it. You are perfectly welcome." And picking up her gloves and hat from the table she left me.

As I walked home my hatred of the wretched piece of metal in my hand increased with every step. I looked at it with disgust when I went to bed that night, and when my glance lighted upon it the next morning I involuntarily shrank from it, as if it had been an evil thing. Over and over again that day I asked myself why I should keep in my possession something which would make my regard for Mildred grow less and less ; which would eventually make me care for her not at all ? The very thought of not caring for Mildred sent a pang through my heart.

My feelings all prompted me to rid myself of what I looked upon as a calamitous talisman, but my reason interfered. If I still wished to marry Janet it was my duty to welcome indifference to Mildred.

In this mood I went out, to stroll, to think, to decide ; and that I might be ready to act on my decision I put the shadrach into my pocket. Without exactly intending it I walked toward the Bronce place, and soon found myself on the edge of a pretty pond which lay at the foot of the garden. Here, in the shade of a tree, there stood a bench, and on this lay a book, an ivory paper-cutter in its leaves as marker.

I knew that Mildred had left that book on the bench ; it was her habit to come to this place to read. As she had not taken the volume with her, it was probable that she intended soon to return. But then the sad thought came to me that if she saw me there she would not return. I picked up the book ; I read the pages she had been reading. As I read I felt that I could think the very thoughts that she thought as she read. I was seized with a yearning to be with her, to read with her, to think with her. Never had my soul gone out to Mildred as at that moment, and yet, heavily dangling in my pocket, I carried—I could not bear to think of it. Seized by a sudden impulse, I put down the book ; I drew out the shadrach, and, tearing off the silver band, I tossed the vile bit of metal into the pond.

"There!" I cried. "Go out of my possession, out of my sight! You shall work no charm on me. Let nature take its course, and let things happen as they may." Then, relieved from the weight on my heart and the weight in my pocket, I went home.

Nature did take its course, and in less than a fortnight from that day the engagement of Janet and Dr. Gilbert was announced. I had done nothing to prevent this, and the news did not disturb my peace of mind ; but my relations with Mildred very much disturbed it. I had hoped that, released from the baleful influence of the shadrach, her friendly feelings toward me would return, and my passion for her had now grown so strong that I waited and watched, as a wrecked mariner waits and watches for the sight of a sail,

for a sign that she had so far softened toward me
that I might dare to speak to her of my love. But
no such sign appeared.

I now seldom visited the Bronce house; no one
of that family, once my best friends, seemed to
care to see me. Evidently Mildred's feelings
toward me had extended themselves to the rest
of the household. This was not surprising, for
her family had long been accustomed to think as ,
Mildred thought.

One day I met Mr. Bronce at the post-office,
and, some other gentlemen coming up, we began to
talk of a proposed plan to introduce a system of
water-works into the village, an improvement much
desired by many of us.

"So far as I am concerned," said Mr. Bronce, " I
am not now in need of anything of the sort. Since
I set up my steam-pump I have supplied my house
from the pond at the end of my garden with all
the water we can possibly want for every purpose."

"Do you mean," asked one of the gentlemen,
" that you get your drinking-water in that way?"

"Certainly," replied Mr. Bronce. " The basin of
the pond is kept as clean and in as good order as

any reservoir can be, and the water comes from an excellent, rapid-flowing spring. I want nothing better."

A chill ran through me as I listened. The shadrach was in that pond. Every drop of water which Mildred drank, which touched her, was influenced by that demoniacal paper-weight, which, without knowing what I was doing, I had thus bestowed upon the whole Bronce family.

When I went home I made diligent search for a stone which might be about the size and weight of the shadrach, and having repaired to a retired spot I practised tossing it as I had tossed the bit of metal into the pond. In each instance I measured the distance which I had thrown the stone, and was at last enabled to make a very fair estimate of the distance to which I had thrown the shadrach when I had buried it under the waters of the pond.

That night there was a half-moon, and between eleven and twelve o'clock, when everybody in our village might be supposed to be in bed and asleep, I made my way over the fields to the back of the Bronce place, taking with me a long fish-cord with a knot in it, showing the average distance to which I had thrown the practice stone. When I reached the pond I stood as nearly as possible in the place by the bench from which I had hurled the shadrach, and to this spot I pegged one end of the cord. I was attired in an old tennis suit, and, having removed my shoes and stockings, I entered the water, holding the roll of cord in my hand. This I slowly unwound as I advanced toward the middle of the pond, and when I reached the knot I stopped, with the water above my waist.

I had found the bottom of the pond very smooth, and free from weeds and mud, and I now began feeling about with my bare feet, as I moved from side to side, describing a small arc; but I discovered nothing more than an occasional pebble no larger than a walnut.

Letting out some more of the cord, I advanced a little farther into the centre of the pond, and slowly described another arc. The water was now nearly up to my armpits, but it was not cold, though if it had been I do not think I should have minded it in the ardour of my search. Suddenly

D

I put my foot on something hard and as big as my fist, but in an instant it moved away from under my foot ; it must have been a turtle. This occurrence made me shiver a little, but I did not swerve from my purpose, and, loosing the string a little more, I went farther into the pond. The water was now nearly up to my chin, and there was something weird, mystical, and awe-inspiring in standing thus in the depths of this silent water, my eyes so near its gently rippling surface, fantastically lighted by the setting moon, and tenanted by nobody knew what cold and slippery creatures. But from side to side I slowly moved, reaching out with my feet in every direction, hoping to touch the thing for which I sought.

Suddenly I set my right foot upon something hard and irregular. Nervously I felt it with my toes. I patted it with my bare sole. It was as big as the shadrach ! It felt like the shadrach. In a few moments I was almost convinced that the direful paper-weight was beneath my foot.

Closing my eyes, and holding my breath, I stooped down into the water, and groped on the bottom with my hands. In some way I had

moved while stooping, and at first I could find
nothing. A sensation of dread came over me as
I felt myself in the midst of the dark solemn
water — around me, above me, everywhere,—
almost suffocated, and apparently deserted even
by the shadrach. But just as I felt that I could
hold my breath no longer, my fingers touched the
thing that had been under my foot, and, clutch-
ing it, I rose and thrust my head out of the water.
I could do nothing until I had taken two or three
long breaths ; then, holding up the object in my
hand to the light of the expiring moon, I saw
that it was like the shadrach ; so like, indeed, that
I felt that it must be it.

Turning, I made my way out of the water as
rapidly as possible, and, dropping on my knees
on the ground, I tremblingly lighted the lantern
which I had left on the bench, and turned its light
on the thing I had found. There must be no
mistake ; if this was not the shadrach I would go
in again. But there was no necessity for re-enter-
ing the pond ; it *was* the shadrach.

With the extinguished lantern in one hand and
the lump of mineral evil in the other, I hurried

home. My wet clothes were sticky and chilly
in the night air. Several times in my haste I
stumbled over clods and briers, and my shoes,
which I had not taken time to tie, flopped up and
down as I ran. But I cared for none of these
discomforts ; the shadrach was in my power.

Crossing a wide field I heard, not far away, the
tramping of hoofs, as of a horseman approaching
at full speed. I stopped and looked in the direction of the sound. My eyes had now become so
accustomed to the dim light that I could distin-
guish objects somewhat plainly, and I quickly
perceived that the animal that was galloping
toward me was a bull. I well knew what bull it
was ; this was Squire Starling's pasture-field, and
that was his great Alderney bull, Ramping Sir.
John of Ramapo II.

I was well acquainted with that bull, renowned
throughout the neighbourhood for his savage
temper and his noble pedigree—son of Ramping
Sir John of Ramapo I., whose sire was the Great
Rodolphin, son of Prince Maximus of Granby, one
of whose daughters averaged eighteen pounds of
butter a week, and who himself had killed two men.

The bull, who had not perceived me when I crossed the field before, for I had then made my way with as little noise as possible, was now bent on punishing my intrusion upon his domains, and bellowed as he came on. I was in a position of great danger. With my flopping shoes it was impossible to escape by flight; I must stand and defend myself. I turned and faced the furious creature, who was not twenty feet distant, and then with all my strength I hurled the shadrach, which I held in my right hand, directly at his shaggy forehead. My ability to project a missile was considerable, for I had held, with credit, the position of pitcher in a base-ball nine, and as the shadrach struck the bull's head with a thud he stopped as if he had suddenly run against a wall.

I do not know that actual and violent contact with the physical organism of a recipient accelerates the influence of a shadrach upon the mental organism of said recipient, but I do know that the contact of my projectile with that bull's skull instantly cooled the animal's fury. For a few moments he stood and looked at me, and then his interest in me as a man and trespasser appeared to fade away, and, moving slowly from me, Ramping Sir John of Ramapo II. began to crop the grass.

I did not stop to look for the shadrach; I considered it safely disposed of. So long as Squire Starling used that field for a pasture, connoisseurs in mineral fragments would not be apt to wander through it, and when it should be ploughed the shadrach, to ordinary eyes no more than a common stone, would be buried beneath the sod. I awoke the next morning refreshed and happy, and none the worse for my wet walk.

" Now," I said to myself, " nature shall truly have her own way. If the uncanny comes into my life and that of those I love, it shall not be brought in by me."

About a week after this I dined with the Bronce family. They were very cordial, and it seemed to me the most natural thing in the world to be sitting at their table. After dinner Mildred and I walked together in the garden. It was a charming evening, and we sat down on the bench by the edge of the pond. I spoke to her of some passages in the book I had once seen there.

" Oh, have you read that ? " she asked with interest.

" I have seen only two pages of it," I said, " and those I read in the volume you left on this bench, with a paper-cutter in it for a marker. I long to read more and talk with you of what I have read."

" Why, then, didn't you wait? You might have known that I would come back."

I did not tell her that I knew that because I was there she would not have come. But before I left the bench I discovered that hereafter, wherever I might be, she was willing to come and stay.

Early in the next spring Mildred and I were married, and on our wedding - trip we passed through a mining district in the mountains. Here we visited one of the great ironworks, and were both interested in witnessing the wonderful power of man, air, and fire over the stubborn king of metals.

" What is this substance ? " asked Mildred of one of the officials who was conducting us through the works.

" That," said the man, " is what we call shad—"

" My dear," I cried, " we must hurry away this

instant or we shall lose the train. Come; quick; there is not a moment for delay." And with a word of thanks to the guide I seized her hand and led her, almost running, into the open air.

Mildred was amazed.

"Never before," she exclaimed, "have I seen you in such a hurry. I thought the train we decided to take did not leave for an hour."

"I have changed my mind," I said, "and think it will be a great deal better for us to take the one which leaves in ten minutes."

ASAPH.

ABOUT a hundred feet back from the main street of a village in New Jersey there stood a very good white house. Half way between it and the sidewalk was a large chestnut tree, which had been the pride of Mr. Himes, who built the house, and was now the pride of Mrs. Himes, his widow, who lived there.

Under the tree was a bench, and on the bench were two elderly men, both smoking pipes, and each one of them leaning forward with his elbows on his knees. One of these, Thomas Rooper by name, was a small man with grey side whiskers, a rather thin face and very good clothes. His pipe was a meerschaum, handsomely coloured, with a long amber tip. He had bought that pipe while on a visit to Philadelphia during the great Centennial Exposition ; and if anyone noticed it and happened to remark what a fine pipe it was, that person would be likely to receive a detailed account of the circumstances of its purchase, with an appendix relating to the Main building, the Art building, the Agricultural building, and many other salient points of the great Exposition which commemorated the centennial of our national independence.

The other man, Asaph Scantle, was of a different type. He was a little older than his companion, but if his hair were grey it did not show very much, as his rather long locks were of a sandy hue and his full face was clean shaven, at least on Wednesdays and Sundays. He was tall, round-shouldered, and his clothes were not good, possessing very evident claims to a position on the retired list. His pipe consisted of a common clay bowl with a long reed stem.

For some minutes the two men continued to puff together as if they were playing a duet upon tobacco pipes, and then Asaph, removing his reed from his lips, remarked, "What you ought to do, Thomas, is to marry money."

"There's sense in that," replied the other, "but you wasn't the first to think of it."

Asaph, who knew very well that Mr. Rooper

never allowed anyone to suppose that he received suggestions from without, took no notice of the last remark, but went on : " Lookin' at the matter in a friendly way, it seems to me it stands to reason that when the shingles on a man's house is so rotten that the rain comes through into every room on the top floor, and when the plaster on the ceilin' is tumblin' down more or less all the time and the window sashes is all loose, and things generally in a condition that he can't let that house without spendin' at least a year's rent on it to git it into decent order, and when a man's got to the time of life——"

" There's nothin' the matter with the time of life," said Thomas ; " that's all right."

" What I was goin' to say was," continued Asaph, " that when a man gits to the time of life when he knows what it is to be comfortable in his mind as well as his body, and that time comes to sensible people as soon as they git fairly growed up, he don't want to give up his good room in the tavern and all the privileges of the house and go to live on his own property and have the plaster come down on his own head and the rain come down on the coverlet of his own bed."

" No, he don't," said Thomas ; " and what is more,

he isn't goin' to do it. But what I git from the rent of that house is what I have to live on ; there's no gittin' around that pint."

"Well, then," said Asaph, " if you don't marry money, what are you goin' to do ? You can't go back to your old business."

"I never had but one business," said Thomas. " I lived with my folks until I was a good deal more than growed up ; and when the war broke out I went as sutler to the rigiment from this place ; and all the money I made I put into my property in the village here. That's what I've lived on ever since. There's no more war, so there's no more sutlers, except away out West, where I wouldn't go ; and there are no more folks, for they are all dead ; and if what Mrs. McJimsey says is true, there'll be no more tenants in my house after the 1st of next November. For when the McJimseys go on account of want of general repairs, it is not to be expected that anybody else will come there. There's nobody in this place that can stand as much as the McJimseys can."

"Consequently," said Asaph, deliberately filling his pipe, " it stands to reason that there ain't nothin' for you to do but marry money."

Thomas Rooper took his pipe from his mouth and sat up straight. Gazing steadfastly at his companion, he remarked, " If you think that is such a good thing to do, why don't you do it yourself? There can't be anybody much harder up than you are."

" The law's agin' my doin' it," said Asaph. " A man can't marry his sister."

" Are you thinking of Marietta Himes ? " asked Mr. Rooper.

" That's the one I'm thinkin' of," said Asaph. " If you can think of anybody better, I'd like you to mention her."

Mr. Rooper did not immediately speak. He presently asked : " What do you call money ? "

" Well," said Asaph, with a little hesitation, " considerin' the circumstances, I should say that in a case like this about $1,500 a year, and a first-rate house, with not a loose shingle on it and not a crack anywhere, and a good garden and an orchard, and two cows and a piece of meadow land on the other side of the creek, and all the clothes a woman need have, is money."

Thomas shrugged his shoulders. " Clothes ! "

he said. " If she marries she'll go out of black, and then she'll have to have new ones, and lots of 'em. That would make a big hole in her money, Asaph."

The other smiled. " I always knowed you was a far-seein' feller, Thomas ; but it stands to reason that Marietta's got a lot of clothes that was on hand before she went into mournin', and she's not the kind of woman to waste 'em. She'll be twistin' 'em about and makin' em over to suit the fashions, and it won't be like her to be buyin' new coloured goods when she's got plenty of 'em already."

There was now another pause in the conversation, and then Mr. Rooper remarked : "Mrs. Himes must be gettin' on pretty well in years."

" She's not a young woman," said Asaph ; " but if she was much younger she wouldn't have you, and if she was much older you wouldn't have her. So it strikes me she's just about the right pint."

" How old was John Himes when he died ?" asked Thomas.

" I don't exactly know that ; but he was a lot older than Marietta." ·

Thomas shook his head. " It strikes me," said

he, "that John Himes had a hearty constitution, and hadn't ought to have died as soon as he did. He fell away a good deal in the last years of his life."

"And considerin' that he died of consumption, he had a right to fall away," said Asaph. "If what you are drivin' at, Thomas, is that Marietta isn't a good housekeeper and hasn't the right sort of notions of feedin', look at me. I've lived with Marietta just about a year, and in that time I have gained forty-two pounds. Now, of course, I ain't unreasonable, and don't mean to say that you would gain forty-two pounds in a year, 'cause you ain't got the frame and bone to put it on; but it wouldn't surprise me a bit if you was to gain twenty or even twenty-five pounds in eighteen months, anyway; and more than that you ought not to ask, Thomas, considerin' your height and general build."

"Isn't Marietta Himes a good deal of a free-thinker?" asked Thomas.

"A what?" cried Asaph. "You mean an infidel?"

"No," said Thomas, "I don't charge people with nothin' more than there's reason for; but they do say that she goes sometimes to one church and sometimes to another, and that if there was a Catholic church in this village she would go to that. And who's goin' to say where a woman will turn up when she don't know her own mind better than that ? "

Asaph coloured a little. " The place where Marietta will turn up," said he warmly, " is on a front seat in the kingdom of heaven ; and if the people that talk about her will mend their ways, they'll see that I am right. You need not trouble yourself about that, Thomas. Marietta Himes is pious to the heel."

Mr. Rooper now shifted himself a little on the bench and crossed one leg over the other. " Now look here, Asaph," he said, with a little more animation than he had yet shown, " supposin' all you say is true, have you got any reason to think that Marietta Himes ain't satisfied with things as they are ? "

" Yes, I have," said Asaph. " And I don't mind tellin' you that the thing she's least satisfied with is me. She wants a man in the house ; that is nateral. She wouldn't be Marietta Himes if she didn't. When I come to live with her I thought the whole business

was settled ; but it isn't. I don't suit her. I don't
say she's lookin' for another man, but if another
man was to come along, and if he was the right
kind of a man, it's my opinion she's ready for him.
I wouldn't say this to everybody, but I say it to
you, Thomas Rooper, 'cause I know what kind of
a man you are."

Mr. Rooper did not return the compliment. " I
don't wonder your sister ain't satisfied with you,"
he said, " for you go ahead of all the lazy men I
ever saw yet. They was sayin' down at the tavern
yesterday, only yesterday, that you could do less
work in more time than anybody they ever before
saw."

" There's two ways of workin'," said Asaph.
" Some people work with their hands and some
with their heads."

Thomas grimly smiled. " It strikes me," said
he, " that the most headwork you do is with your
jaws."

Asaph was not the man to take offence readily,
especially when he considered it against his interest
to do so, and he showed no resentment at this remark. " ' Tain't so much my not makin' myself more

E

generally useful," he said, "that Marietta objects
to ; though, of course, it could not be expected that
a man that hasn't got any interest in property
would keep workin' at it like a man that has got
an interest in it, such as Marietta's husband would
have ; but it's my general appearance that she don't
like. She's told me more than once she didn't so
much mind my bein' lazy as lookin' lazy."

"I don't wonder she thinks that way," said
Thomas. "But look here, Asaph, do you suppose
that if Marietta Himes was to marry a man he
would really come into her property?"

"There ain't nobody that knows my sister better
than I know her, and I can say, without any fear
of bein' contradicted, that when she gives herself
to a man the good-will and fixtures will be included."

Thomas Rooper now leaned forward with his
elbows on his knees without smoking, and Asaph
Scantle leaned forward with his elbows on his
knees without smoking. And thus they remained,
saying nothing to each other for the space of some
ten minutes.

Asaph was a man who truly used his head a great

deal more than he used his hands. He had always been a shiftless fellow, but he was no fool, and this his sister found out soon after she asked him to come and make his home with her. She had not done this because she wanted a man in the house, for she had lived two or three years without that convenience and had not felt the need of it. But she heard that Asaph was in very uncomfortable circumstances, and she had sent for him solely for his own good. The arrangement proved to be a very good one for her brother, but not a good one for her. She had always known that Asaph's head was his main dependence, but she was just beginning to discover that he liked to use his head so that other people's hands should work for him.

"There ain't nobody comin' to see your sister, is there?" asked Thomas, suddenly.

"Not a livin' soul," said Asaph, "except women, married folk and children. But it has always surprised me that nobody did come; but just at this minute the field's clear and the gate's open."

"Well," said Mr. Rooper, "I'll think about it."

"That's right," said Asaph, rubbing his knees with his hands. "That's right. But now tell me

E 2

Thomas Rooper, supposin' you get Marietta, what are you goin' to do for me?"

"For you?" exclaimed the other. "What have you got to do with it?"

"A good deal," said Asaph. "If you get Marietta with her $1,500 a year, and it wouldn't surprise me if it was $1,800, and her house and her garden and her cattle and her field and her furniture, which I didn't mention before, with not a leg loose nor a cushion scratched, you will get her because I proposed her to you, and because I backed you up afterward. And now then, I want to know what you are goin' to do for me."

"What do you want?" asked Thomas.

"The first thing I want," said Asaph, "is a suit of clothes. These clothes is disgraceful."

"You are right there," said Mr. Rooper. "I wonder your sister lets you come around in front of the house. But what do you mean by clothes; winter clothes or summer clothes?"

"Winter," said Asaph, without hesitation. "I don't count summer clothes. And when I say a suit of clothes, I mean shoes and hat and under-clothes."

Mr. Rooper gave a sniff. " I wonder you don't say overcoat," he remarked.

" I do say overcoat," replied Asaph. "A suit of winter clothes is a suit of clothes that you can go out into the weather in without missin' nothin'."

Mr. Rooper smiled sarcastically. " Is there anything else you want ? " he asked.

" Yes," said Asaph, decidedly, " there is. I want an umbrella."

" Cotton or silk ? "

Asaph hesitated. He had never had a silk umbrella in his hand in his life. He was afraid to strike too high, and he answered, " I want a good stout gingham."

Mr. Rooper nodded his head. " Very good," he said. "And is that all ? "

" No," said Asaph, " it ain't all. There is one more thing I want, and that is a dictionary."

The other man rose to his feet, " Upon my word," he exclaimed, " I never before saw a man that would sell his sister for a dictionary. And what you want with a dictionary is past my conceivin'."

" Well, it ain't past mine," said Asaph. " For

more than ten years I have wanted a dictionary. If I had a dictionary I could make use of my head in a way that I can't now. There is books in this house, but amongst 'em there is no dictionary. If there had been one, I'd been a different man by this time from what I am now, and like as not Marietta wouldn't have wanted any other man in the house but me."

Mr. Rooper stood looking upon the ground ; and Asaph, who had also arisen, waited for him to speak. "You are a graspin' man, Asaph," said Thomas. "But there is another thing I'd like to know : if I give you them clothes, you don't want them before she's married ? "

"Yes, I do," said Asaph. "If I come to the weddin', I can't wear these things. I have got to have them first."

Mr. Rooper gave his head a little twist. "There's many a slip 'twixt the cup and the lip," said he.

"Yes," said Asaph ; " and there's different cups and different lips. But what's more, if I was to be best man, which would be nateral, considerin' I'm your friend and her brother, you wouldn't want me standin' up in this rig. And that's puttin' it in your own point of view, Thomas."

"It strikes me," said the other, "that I could get a best man that would furnish his own clothes ; but we will see about that. There's another thing, Asaph," he said abruptly, "what are Mrs. Himes's views concernin' pipes ? "

This question startled and frightened Asaph. He knew that his sister could not abide the smell of tobacco, and that Mr. Rooper was an inveterate smoker.

"That depends," said he, "on the kind of tobacco. I don't mind sayin' that Marietta isn't partial to the kind of tobacco I smoke. But I ain't a moneyed man, and I can't afford to buy nothin' but cheap stuff. But when it comes to a meerschaum pipe and the very finest Virginia or North Carolina smoking tobacco, such as a moneyed man would be likely to use——"

At this moment there came from the house the sound of a woman's voice, not loud, but clear and distinct, and it said "Asaph."

This word sent through Mr. Rooper a gentle thrill such as he did not remember ever having felt before. There seemed to be in it a suggestion, a sort of prophecy, of what appeared to him as an undefined and chaotic bliss. He was not a fanciful man, but he could not help imagining himself standing alone under that chestnut tree and that voice calling " Thomas."

Upon Asaph the effect was different. The interruption was an agreeable one in one way, because it cut short his attempted explanation of the tobacco question ; but in another way he knew that it meant the swinging of an axe, and that was not pleasant.

Mr. Rooper walked back to the tavern in a cogitative state of mind. " That Asaph Scantle," he said to himself, " has got a headpiece, there's no denying it. If it had not been for him I do not believe I should have thought of his sister ; at least not until the McJimseys had left my house, and then it might have been too late."

Marietta Himes was a woman with a gentle voice and an appearance and demeanour indicative of a general softness of disposition, but beneath this mild exterior there was a great deal of firmness of purpose. Asaph had not seen very much of his

sister since she had grown up and married ; and
when he came to live with her he thought that he
was going to have things pretty much his own way.
But it was not long before he entirely changed his
mind.

Mrs. Himes was of moderate height, pleasant
countenance, and a figure inclined to plumpness.
Her dark hair, in which there was not a line of
gray, was brushed down smoothly on each side of
her face, and her dress, while plain, was extremely
neat.   In fact, everything in the house and on the
place was extremely neat, except Asaph.

She was in the bright little dining-room which
looked out on the flower garden, preparing the
table for supper, placing every plate, dish, glass, and
cup with as much care and exactness as if a civil
engineer had drawn a plan on the tablecloth, with
places marked for the position of each article.

As she finished her work by placing a chair on
each side of the table, a quiet smile, the result of
a train of thought in which she had been indulging
for the past half-hour, stole over her face.   She
passed through the kitchen, with a glance at the
stove to see if the tea-kettle had begun to boil, and

going out of the back door, she walked over to the shed where her brother was splitting kindling wood.

"Asaph," said Mrs. Himes, "if I were to give you a good suit of clothes, would you promise me that you would never smoke when wearing them?"

Her brother looked at her in amazement. "Clothes!" he repeated.

"Mr. Himes was about your size," said his sister, "and he left a good many clothes, which are most of them very good and carefully packed away, so that I am sure there is not a moth hole in any one of them. I have several times thought, Asaph, that I might give you some of his clothes ; but it did seem to me a desecration to have the clothes of such a man, who was so particular and nice, filled and saturated with horrible tobacco smoke which he detested. But now you are getting to be so awful shabby, I do not see how I can stand it any longer. But one thing I will not do, I will not have Mr. Himes's clothes smelling of tobacco as yours do, and not only your own tobacco but Mr. Rooper's."

"I think," said Asaph, "that you are not exactly

right just there. What you smell about me is my smoke. Thomas Rooper never uses anything but the finest scented and delicatest brands. I think that if you come to get used to his tobacco smoke you would like it. But as to my takin' off my clothes and puttin' on a different suit every time I want to light my pipe, that's pretty hard lines, it seems to me."

"It would be a good deal easier to give up the pipe," said his sister.

"I will do that," said Asaph, "when you give up tea. But you know as well as I do that there's no use of either of us a-tryin' to change our comfortable habits at our time of life."

"I kept on hoping," said Mrs. Himes, "that you would feel yourself that you were not fit to be seen by decent people, and that you would go to work and earn at least enough money to buy yourself some clothes. But as you don't seem inclined to do that, I thought I would make you this offer. But you must understand that I will not have you smoke in Mr. Himes's clothes."

Asaph stood thinking, the head of his axe resting upon the ground, a position which suited him. He was in a little perplexity. Marietta's proposition seemed to interfere somewhat with the one he had made to Thomas Rooper. Here was a state of affairs which required most careful consideration. "I've been arrangin' about some clothes," he said presently, "for I know very well I need 'em; but I don't know just yet how it will turn out."

"I hope, Asaph," said Marietta quickly, "that you are not thinking of going into debt for clothing, and I know that you haven't been working to earn money. What arrangements have you been making?"

"That's my private affair," said Asaph, "but there's no debt in it. It is all fair and square— cash down, so to speak; though, of course, it's not cash, but work. But, as I said before, that isn't settled."

"I am afraid, Asaph," said his sister, "that if you have to do the work first you will never get the clothes, and so you might as well come back to my offer."

Asaph came back to it and thought about it very earnestly. If by any chance he could get two suits of clothes, he would then feel that he had a head worth having. "What would you say," he said presently, "if when I wanted to smoke I was to put on a long duster—I guess Mr. Himes had dusters—and a nightcap and rubbers? I'd agree to hang the duster and the cap in the shed here and never smoke without putting 'em on." There was a deep purpose in this proposition, for, enveloped in the long duster, he might sit with Thomas Rooper under the chestnut tree and smoke and talk and plan as long as he pleased, and his companion would not know that he did not need a new suit of clothes.

"Nonsense," said Mrs. Himes; "you must make up your mind to act perfectly fairly, Asaph, or else say you will not accept my offer. But if you don't accept it, I can't see how you can keep on living with me."

"What do you mean by clothes, Marietta?" he asked.

"Well, I mean a complete suit, of course," said she.

"Winter or summer?"

"I hadn't thought of that," Mrs. Himes replied, "but that can be as you choose."

"Overcoat?" asked Asaph.

"Yes," said she, "and cane and umbrella, if you like, and pocket-hankerchiefs too. I will fit you out completely, and shall be glad to have you looking like a decent man."

At the mention of the umbrella another line of perplexity showed itself upon Asaph's brow. The idea came to him that if she would add a dictionary he would strike a bargain. Thomas Rooper was certainly a very undecided and uncertain sort of man. But then there came up the thought of his pipe, and he was all at sea again. Giving up smoking was almost the same as giving up eating. "Marietta," said he, "I will think about this."

"Very well," she answered, "but it's my opinion, Asaph, that you ought not to take more than one minute to think about it. However, I will give you until to-morrow morning, and then if you decide that you don't care to look like a respectable citizen, I must have some further talk with you about our future arrangements."

"Make it to-morrow night," said Asaph. And his sister consented.

The next day Asaph was unusually brisk and

active ; and very soon after breakfast he walked over to the village tavern to see Mr. Rooper.

" Hello ! " exclaimed that individual, surprised at his visitor's early appearance at the business centre of the village. " What's started you out ? Have you come after them clothes ? "

A happy thought struck Asaph. He had made this visit with the intention of feeling his way towards some decision on the important subject of his sister's proposition, and here a way seemed to be opened to him. " Thomas," said he, taking his friend aside, " I am in an awful fix. Marietta can't stand my clothes any longer. If she can't stand them she can't stand me, and when it comes to that, you can see for yourself that I can't help you."

A shade settled upon Mr. Rooper's face. During the past evening he had been thinking and puffing, and puffing and thinking until everybody else in the tavern had gone to bed, and he had finally made up his mind that, if he could do it, he would marry Marietta Himes. He had never been very intimate with her or her husband, but he had been to meals in the house, and he remembered the fragrant coffee and the light, puffy, well-baked rolls made by Marietta's own hands; and he thought of the many differences between living in that very good house with that gentle, pleasant-voiced lady and his present life in the village tavern.

And so, having determined that without delay he would, with the advice and assistance of Asaph, begin his courtship, it was natural that he should feel a shock of discouragement when he heard Asaph's announcement that his sister could not endure him in the house any longer. To attack that house and its owner without the friendly offices upon which he depended was an undertaking for which he was not at all prepared.

" I don't wonder at her," he said, sharply, " not a bit. But this puts a mighty different face on the thing what we talked about yesterday."

" It needn't," said Asaph, quietly. " The clothes you was goin' to give me wouldn't cost a cent more to-day than they would in a couple of months, say ; and when I've got 'em on Marietta will be glad to have me around. Everything can go on just as we bargained for,"

Thomas shook his head. " That would be a mighty resky piece of business," he said. " You would be all right, but that's not sayin' that I would ; for it strikes me that your sister is about as much a bird in the bush as any flyin' critter."

Asaph smiled. " If the bush was in the middle of a field," said he, " and there was only one boy after the bird, it would be a pretty tough job. But if the bush is in the corner of two high walls, and there's two boys, and one of 'em's got a fish-net what he can throw clean over the bush, why, then the chances is a good deal better. But droppin' figgers, Thomas, and speakin' plain and straight-forward, as I always do——"

" About things you want to git," interrupted Thomas.

" About everything," resumed Asaph. " I'll just tell you this : if I don't git decent clothes now, to-day, or perhaps to-morrow, I have got to travel out of Marietta's house. I can do it, and she knows it. I can go back to Drummondville, and git my board for keepin' books in the store, and nobody there cares what sort of clothes I wear. But when

F

that happens, your chances of gittin' Marietta goes up higher than a kite."

To the mind of Mr. Rooper this was most conclusive reasoning ; but he would not admit it, and he did not like it. " Why don't your sister give you clothes ? " he said. " Old Himes must have left some."

A thin chill like a needleful of frozen thread ran down Asaph's back. " Mr. Himes's clothes ! " he exclaimed. "What in the world are you talkin' about, Thomas Rooper ? 'Tain't likely he had many 'cept what he was buried in, and what's left, if there is any, Marietta would no more think of givin' away than she would of hangin' up his funeral wreath for the canary bird to perch on. There's a room up in the garret where she keeps his special things, for she's awful particular, and if there is any of his clothes up there I expect she's got 'em framed."

" If she thinks as much of him as that," muttered Mr. Rooper.

" Now don't git any sech ideas as them into your head, Thomas," said Asaph, quickly. " Marietta ain't a woman to rake up the past,

and you never need be afraid of her rakin' up
Mr. Himes. All of the premises will be hern and
yourn, except that room in the garret, and it ain't
likely she'll ever ask you to go in there."

"The Lord knows I won't want to," ejaculated
Mr. Rooper.

The two men walked slowly to the end of a line
of well-used, or, rather, badly-used wooden arm-
chairs which stood upon the tavern piazza, and
seated themselves. Mr. Rooper's mind was in a
highly perturbed condition. If he accepted
Asaph's present proposition he would have to
make a considerable outlay with a very shadowy
prospect of return.

"If you haven't got the ready money for the
clothes," said Asaph, after having given his companion some minutes for silent consideration,
"there ain't a man in this village what they would
trust sooner at the store for clothes," and then
after a pause he added, "or books, which, of course,
they can order from town."

At this Mr. Roper simply shrugged his shoulders.
The question of ready money or credit did not
trouble him.

F 2

At this moment a man in a low phaeton, drawn by a stout grey horse, passed the tavern.

"Who's that?" asked Asaph, who knew everybody in the village.

"That's Doctor Wicker," said Thomas. "He lives over at Timberley. He 'tended John Himes in his last sickness."

"He don't practise here, does he?" said Asaph. "I never see him."

"No; but he was called in to consult." And then the speaker dropped again into cogitation.

After a few minutes Asaph rose. He knew that Thomas Rooper had a slow-working mind, and thought it would be well to leave him to himself for awhile. "I'll go home," said he, "and 'tend to my chores, and by the time you feel like comin' up and takin' a smoke with me under the chestnut tree, I reckon you will have made up your mind, and we'll settle this thing. Fer if I have got to go back to Drummondville, I s'pose I'll have to pack up this afternoon."

"If you'd say pack off instead of pack up," remarked the other, "you'd come nearer the facts, considerin' the amount of your personal property. But I'll be up there in an hour or two."

When Asaph came within sight of his sister's house he was amazed to see a phaeton and a grey horse standing in front of the gate. From this it was easy to infer that the doctor was in the house. What on earth could have happened? Was anything the matter with Marietta? And if so, why did she send for a physician who lived at a distance, instead of Doctor McIlvaine, the village doctor? In a very anxious state of mind Asaph reached the gate, and irresolutely went into the yard. His impulse was to go to the house and see what had happened: but he hesitated. He felt that Marietta might object to having a comparative stranger know that such an exceedingly shabby fellow was her brother. And, besides, his sister could not have been overtaken by any sudden illness. She had always appeared perfectly well, and there would have been no time during his brief absence from the house to send over to Timberley for a doctor.

So he sat down under the chestnut tree to consider this strange condition of affairs. "Whatever it is," he said to himself, "it's nothin' suddint and it's bound to be chronic, and that'll skeer Thomas.

I wish I hadn't asked him to come up here. The best thing for me to do will be to pretend that I have been sent to get something at the store, and go straight back and keep him from comin' up."

But Asaph was a good deal quicker to think than to move, and he still sat with brows wrinkled and mind beset by doubts. For a moment he thought that it might be well to accept Marietta's proposition and let Thomas go ; but then he remembered the conditions, and he shut his mental eyes at the prospect.

At that moment the gate opened and in walked Thomas Rooper. He had made up his mind and had come to say so ; but the sight of the phaeton and grey horse caused him to postpone his intended announcement. " What's Doctor Wicker doin' here ? " he asked, abruptly.

" Dunno," said Asaph, as carelessly as he could speak. " I don't meddle with household matters of that kind. I expect it somethin' the matter with that girl Betsey that Marietta hires to help her. She's always wrong some way or other, so that she can't do her own proper work, which I know, havin' to do a good deal of it myself. I expect it's rickets, like as not. Gals do have that sort of thing, don't they?"

" Never had anything to do with sick gals," said Thomas, "or sick people of any sort, and don't want to. But it must be somethin' pretty deep-seated for your sister to send all the way to Timberley for a doctor."

Asaph knew very well that Mrs. Himes was too economical a person to think of doing such a thing as that, and he knew also that Betsey was as good a specimen of rustic health as could be found in the county. And therefore his companion's statement that he wanted to have nothing to do with sick people had for him a saddening import.

" I settled that business of yourn," said Mr. Rooper, " pretty soon after you left me. I thought I might as well come round and tell you about it. I'll make you a fair and square offer. I'll give you them clothes, though it strikes me that winter goods will be pretty heavy for this time of year ; but it will be on this condition : if I don't get Marietta, you have got to give 'em back."

Asaph smiled.

"I know what you are grinnin' at," said Thomas; "but you needn't think that you are goin' to have the wearin' of them clothes for two or three months and then give 'em back, I don't go in for any long courtships. What I do in that line will be short and sharp."

"How short?" asked Asaph.

"Well, this is Thursday," replied the other, "and I calculate to ask her on Monday."

Asaph looked at his companion in amazement. "By George!" he exclaimed, "that won't work. Why, it took Marietta more'n five days to make up her mind whether she would have the chicken-house painted green or red, and you can't expect her to be quicker than that in takin' a new husband. She'd say No just as certain as she would now if you was to go in and ask her right before the doctor and Betsey. And I'll just tell you plain that it wouldn't pay me to do all the hustlin' around and talkin' and argyin' and recom-mendin' that I'd have to do just for the pleasure of wearin' a suit of warm clothes for four July days. I tell you what it is, it won't do to spring that sort of thing on a woman, especially when she's what you might call a trained widder. You got to give 'em time to think over the matter and to look up your references. There's no use talkin' about it; you must give 'em time, especially when the offer comes from a person that nobody but me has ever thought of as a marryin' man."

"Humph!" said Thomas. "That's all you know about it."

"Facts is facts, and you can't git around 'em. There isn't a woman in this village what wouldn't take at least two weeks to git it into her head that you was really courtin' her. She would be just as likely to think that you was trying' to get a tenant in place of the McJimseys. But a month of your courtin' and a month of my workin' would just about make the matter all right with Marietta, and then you could sail in and settle it."

"Very good," said Mr. Rooper, rising suddenly. "I will court your sister for one month; and if on the 17th day of August she takes me, you can go up to the store and git them clothes; but you can't do it one minute afore. Good mornin'."

Asaph, left alone, heaved a sigh. He did not

despair ; but truly, fate was heaping a great many obstacles in his path. He thought it was a very hard thing for a man to get his rights in this world.

Mrs. Himes sat on one end of a black hair-covered sofa in the parlour, and Doctor Wicker sat on a black hair-covered chair opposite to her and not far away. The blinds of the window opening upon the garden were drawn up ; but those on the front window, which commanded a view of the chestnut tree, were down. Doctor Wicker had just made a proposal of marriage to Mrs. Himes, and at that moment they were both sitting in silence.

The doctor, a bluff, hearty-looking man of about forty-five, had been very favourably impressed by Mrs. Himes when he first made her acquaintance, during her husband's sickness, and since that time he had seen her occasionally and had thought about her a great deal. Latterly letters had passed between them, and now he had come to make his declaration in person.

It was true, as her brother had said, that Marietta was not quick in making up her mind. But in this case she was able to act more promptly than usual because she had in a great measure settled this

matter before the arrival of the doctor. She knew
he was going to propose, and she was very much
inclined to accept him. This it was which had
made her smile when she was setting the table the
afternoon before, and this it was which had prompted
her to make her proposition to her brother in regard to his better personal appearance.

But now she was in a condition of nervous trepi-
dation and made no answer. The doctor thought
this was natural enough under the circumstances,
but he had no idea of the cause of it. The cause
of it was sitting under the chestnut tree, the bright
sunlight, streaming through a break in the branches
above, illuminating and emphasising and exagger-
ating his extreme shabbiness. The doctor had
never seen Asaph, and it would have been a great
shock to Marietta's self-respect to have him see her
brother in his present aspect.

Through a crack in the blind of the front window
she had seen Asaph come in and sit down, and
she had seen Mr. Rooper arrive and had noticed
his departure. And now, with an anxiety which
made her chin tremble, she sat and hoped that
Asaph would get up and go away. For she knew

that if she should say to the doctor what she was perfectly willing to say then and there, he would very soon depart, being a man of practical mind and pressing business ; and that, going to the front door with him, she would be obliged to introduce him to a prospective brother-in-law whose appearance, she truly believed, would make him sick. For the doctor was a man, she well knew, who was quite as nice and particular about dress and personal appearance as the late Mr. Himes had been.

Doctor Wicker, aware that the lady's perturbation was increasing instead of diminishing, thought it wise not to press the matter at this moment. He felt that he had been, perhaps, a little over-prompt in making his proposition. "Madam," said he, rising, "I will not ask you to give me an answer now. I will go away and let you think about it and will come again to-morrow."

Through the crack in the window-blind Marietta saw that Asaph was still under the tree. What could she do to delay the doctor? She did not offer to take leave of him, but stood looking upon the floor. It seemed a shame to make so good a man go all the way back to Timberley and come again next day, just because that ragged, dirty Asaph was sitting under the chestnut tree.

The doctor moved toward the door, and as she followed him she glanced once more through the crack in the window-blind, and, to her intense delight, she saw Asaph jump up from the bench and run around to the side of the house. He had heard the doctor's footsteps in the hallway, and had not wished to meet him. The unsatisfactory condition of his outward appearance had been so strongly impressed upon him of late that he had become a little sensitive in regard to it when strangers were concerned. But if he had only known that his exceedingly unattractive garments had prevented his sister from making a compact which would have totally ruined his plans in regard to her matrimonial disposition and his own advantage, he would have felt for those old clothes the respect and gratitude with which a Roman soldier regarded the shield and sword which had won him a battle.

Down the middle of the garden, at the back of the house, there ran a path, and along this path Asaph walked meditatively, with his hands in his trousers' pockets. It was a discouraging place for him to walk, for the beds on each side of him were full of weeds, which he had intended to pull out as soon as he should find time for the work, but which had now grown so tall and strong that they could not be rooted up without injuring the plants which were the legitimate occupants of the garden.

Asaph did not know it, but at this moment there was not one person in the whole world who thought kindly of him. His sister was so mortified by him that she was in tears in the house. His crony, Thomas, had gone away almost angry with him, and even Betsey, whom he had falsely accused of rickets, and who had often shown a pity for him simply because he looked so forlorn, had steeled her heart against him that morning when she found he had gone away without providing her with any fuel for the kitchen fire.

But he had not made a dozen turns up and down the path before he became aware of the feeling of Marietta. She looked out of the back door and then walked rapidly toward him. "Asaph," said she, "I hope you are considering what I said to you yesterday, for I mean to stick to my word. If you don't choose to accept my offer, I want you to go back to Drummondville early to-morrow morning. And I don't feel in the least as if I were turning you out of the house, for I have given you a chance to stay here and have only asked you to act like a decent Christian. I will not have you here disgracing my home. When Doctor Wicker came to-day, and I looked out and saw you with that miserable little coat with the sleeves half-way up to the elbows and great holes in it which you will not let anybody patch, because you are too proud to wear patches, and those wretched faded trousers, out at the knees, and which have been turned up and hemmed at the bottom so often that they are six inches above your shoes, and your whole scarcrow appearance, I was so ashamed of you that I could not keep the tears out of my eyes. To tell a respectable gentleman like Doctor Wicker that you were my brother was more than I could bear; and I was glad when I saw you get up and sneak out of the way. I hate to talk to you in this way, Asaph, but you have brought it on yourself."

Her brother looked at her a moment. " Do

you want me to go away before breakfast?" he said.

"No," answered Marietta, "but immediately afterward." And in her mind she resolved that breakfast should be very early the next morning.

If Asaph had any idea of yielding he did not intend to show it until the last moment, and so he changed the subject. "What's the matter with Betsey?" said he. "If she's out of health you'd better get rid of her."

"There's nothing the matter with Betsey," answered his sister. "Doctor Wicker came to see me."

"Came to see you!" exclaimed her brother. "What in the world did he do that for? you never told me that you were ailin'. Is it that sprain in your ankle?"

"Nonsense," said Marietta. "I had almost recovered from that sprain when you came here. There's nothing the matter with my ankle, the trouble is probably with my heart."

The moment she said this she regretted it, for Asaph had such a good head, and could catch meanings so quickly.

" I'm sorry to hear that, Marietta," said Asaph.
" That's a good deal more serious."

"Yes," said she. And she turned and went
back to the house.

Asaph continued to walk up and down the path.
He had not done a stroke of work that morning,
but he did not think of that. His sister's communication saddened him. He liked Marietta,
and it grieved him to hear that she had anything
the matter with her heart. He knew that that
often happened to people who looked perfectly
well, and there was no reason why he should have
suspected any disorder in her. Of course, in this
case, there was good reason for her sending for
the very best doctor to be had. It was all plain
enough to him now.

But as he walked and walked and walked, and
looked at the garden and looked at the little
orchard and looked at the house and the top of
the big chestnut tree, which showed itself above
the roof, a thought came into his mind which had
never been there before—he was Marietta's heir.
It was a dreadful thing to think of his sister's
possible early departure from this world; but after

G

all, life is life, reality is reality, and business is business. He was Marietta's only legal heir.

Of course he had known this before, but it had never seemed to be of any importance. He was a good deal older than she was, and he had always looked upon her as a marrying woman. When he made his proposition to Mr. Rooper the thought of his own heirship never came into his mind. In fact, if anyone had offered him ten dollars for said heirship he would have asked fifteen and would have afterward agreed to split the difference and take twelve and a half.

But now everything had changed. If Marietta had anything the matter with her heart, there was no knowing when all that he saw might be his own. No sooner had he walked and thought long enough for his mind to fully appreciate the altered aspects of his future than he determined to instantly thrust out Mr. Rooper from all connection with that future. He would go and tell him so at once.

To the dismay of Betsey, who had been watching him, expecting that he would soon stop walking about and go and saw some wood with which to cook the dinner, he went out of the front gate and strode rapidly into the village. He had some trouble in finding Mr. Rooper, who had gone off to take a walk and arrange a conversation with which to begin his courtship of Mrs. Himes, but he overtook him under a tree by the side of the creek. "Thomas," said he, " I have changed my mind about that business between us. You have been very hard on me, and I'm not goin' to stand it. I can get the clothes and things I need without makin' myself your slave and workin' myself to death, and, perhaps, settin' my sister agin me for life by tryin' to make her believe that black's white, that you are the kind of husband she ought to have, and that you hate pipes and never touch spirits. It would be a mean thing for me to do and I won't do it. I did think you were a generous-minded man with the right sort of feeling for them as wanted to be your friends, but I have found out that I was mistook, and I'm not goin' to sacrifice my sister to any such person. Now that's my state of mind plain and square."

Thomas Rooper shrunk two inches in height.

"Asaph Scantle," he said, in a voice which seemed also to have shrunk, "I don't understand you. I wasn't hard on you. I only wanted to make a fair bargain. If I'd got her I'd paid up cash on delivery. You couldn't expect a man to do more than that. But I tell you, Asaph, that I am mighty serious about this. The more I have thought about your sister the more I want her. And when I tell you that I've been a-thinkin' about her pretty much all night you may know that I want her a good deal. And I was intendin' to go to-morrow and begin to court her."

"Well, you needn't," said Asaph. "It won't do no good. If you don't have me to back you up you might as well try to twist that tree as to move her. You can't do it."

"But you don't mean to go agin me, do you, Asaph?" asked Thomas, ruefully.

"'Taint necessary," replied the other. "You will go agin yourself."

For a few moments Mr. Rooper remained silent. He was greatly discouraged and dismayed by what had been said to him, but he could not yet

give up what had become the great object of his
life. "Asaph," said he, presently, "it cuts me to
the in'ards to think that you have gone back on
me ; but I tell you what I'll do, if you will promise
not to say anything agin me to Mrs. Himes, and
not to set yourself in any way between me and
her, I'll go along with you to the store now and
you can git that suit of clothes and the umbrella,
and I'll tell 'em to order the dictionary and hand
it over to you as soon as it comes. I'd like you
to help me, but if you will only promise to stand
out of the way and not hinder, I'll do the fair
thing by you and pay in advance."

"Humph !" said Asaph. "I do believe you
think you are the only man that wants Marietta."

A pang passed through the heart of Mr.
Rooper. He had been thinking a great deal of
Mrs. Himes and everything connected with her,
and he had even thought of that visit of Doctor
Wicker's. That gentleman was a widower and a
well-to-do and well-appearing man ; and it would
have been a long way for him to come just for
some trifling rickets in a servant girl. Being
really in love, his imagination was in a very

capering mood, and he began to fear that the doctor had come to court Mrs. Himes. " Asaph," he said quickly, "that's a good offer I make you. If you take it, in less than an hour you can walk home looking like a gentleman."

Asaph had taken his reed pipe from his coat pocket and was filling it. As he pushed the coarse tobacco into the bowl, he considered. " Thomas," said he, "that ain't enough. Things have changed, and it wouldn't pay me. But I won't be hard on you. I'm a good friend of yourn and I'll tell you what I'll do. If you will give me now all the things we spoke of between us—and I forgot to mention a cane and pocket hankerchiefs—and give me, besides, that meerschaum pipe of yourn, I'll promise not to hinder you, but let you go ahead and git Marietta if you kin. I must say it's a good deal for me to do, knowin' how much you'll git and how little you'll give, and knowin', too, the other chances she's got if she wanted 'em ; but I'll do it for the sake of friendship."

" My meerschaum pipe ! " groaned Mr. Rooper. " My Centennial Exhibition pipe ! " His tones

were so plaintive that for a moment Asaph felt a
little touch of remorse. But then he reflected that
if Thomas really did get Marietta the pipe would
be of no use to him, for she would not allow him
to smoke it. And, besides, realities were realities
and business was business. " That pipe may be
very dear to you," he said, "Thomas, but I want
you to remember that Marietta's very dear to
me."

This touched Mr. Rooper, whose heart was
sensitive as it had never been before. "Come
along, Asaph," he said. "You shall have everything, meerschaum pipe included. If anybody but
me is going to smoke that pipe I'd like it to be my
brother-in-law." Thus, with amber-tipped guile
Mr. Rooper hoped to win over his friend to not
only not hinder, but to help him.

As the two men walked away, Asaph thought
that he was not acting an unfraternal part toward
Marietta, for it would not be necessary for him to
say or do anything to induce her to refuse so un-
suitable a suitor as Thomas Rooper.

About fifteen minutes before dinner—which had
been cooked with bits of wood which Betsey had

picked up here and there — was ready, Asaph walked into the front yard of his sister's house attired in a complete suit of new clothes, thick and substantial in texture, pepper-and-salt in colour, and as long in the legs and arms as the most fastidious could desire. He had on a new shirt and a clean collar, with a handsome black silk cravat tied in a great bow, and a new felt hat was on his head. On his left arm he carried an overcoat, carefully folded with the lining outside, and in his right hand an umbrella and a cane. In his pockets were half a dozen new handkerchiefs and the case containing Mr. Rooper's Centennial meerschaum.

Marietta, who was in the hallway when he opened the front door, scarcely knew him as he approached. "Asaph!" she exclaimed. "What has happened to you? Why, you actually look like a gentleman!"

Asaph grinned. "Do you want me to go to Drummondville right after breakfast to-morrow?" he asked.

"My dear brother," said Marietta, "don't crush me by talking about that. But if you could have seen yourself as I saw you, and could have felt as I

felt, you would not wonder at me. You must forget all that. I should be proud now to introduce
you as my brother to any doctor or king or presi-
dent. But tell me how you got those beautiful
clothes."

Asaph was sometimes beset by an absurd regard
for truth, which much annoyed him. He could
not say that he had worked for the clothes, and he
did not wish his sister to think that he had run in
debt for them. " They're paid for, every thread
of 'em," he said. " I got 'em in trade. These
things is mine, and I don't owe no man a cent for
'em ; and it seems to me that dinner must be
ready."

" And proud I am," said Marietta, who never
before had shown such enthusiastic affection for
her brother, " to sit down to the table with such a
nice-looking fellow as you are."

The next morning Mr. Rooper came into Mrs.
Himes's yard and there beheld Asaph in all the
glory of his new clothes sitting under the chestnut
tree smoking the Centennial meerschaum pipe.
Mr. Rooper himself was dressed in his very best
clothes, but he carried with him no pipe.

"Sit down," said Asaph, "and have a smoke."

"No," replied the other, "I am goin' in the house. I have come to see your sister."

"Goin' to begin already?" said Asaph.

"Yes," said the other, "I told you I was going to begin to-day."

"Very good," said his friend, crossing his pepper-and-salt legs, "and you will finish the 17th of August. That's a good reasonable time."

But Mr. Rooper had no intention of courting Mrs. Himes for a month. He intended to propose to her that very morning. He had been turning over the matter in his mind, and for several reasons had come to this conclusion In the first place, he did not believe that he could trust Asaph, even for a single day, not to oppose him. Furthermore, his mind was in such a turmoil from the combined effect of the constantly present thought that Asaph was wearing his clothes, his hat, and his shoes, and smoking his beloved pipe, and of the perplexities and agitations consequent upon his sentiments toward Mrs. Himes, that he did not believe he could bear the mental strain during another night.

Five minutes later Marietta Himes was sitting

on the horse-hair sofa in the parlour with Mr.
Rooper on the horse-hair chair opposite to her and
not very far away, and he was delivering the
address which he had prepared.

" Madam," said he, " I am a man that takes
things in this world as they comes, and is content
to wait until the time comes for them to come. I
was well acquainted with John Himes. I knowed
him in life and I helped lay him out. As long as
there was reason to suppose that the late Mr.
Himes—I mean that the grass over the grave of
Mr. Himes had remained unwithered, I am not the
man to take one step in the direction of his shoes,
nor even to consider the size of 'em in connection
with the measure of my own feet. But time will
pass on in nater as well as in real life ; and while I
know very well, Mrs. Himes, that certain feelin's
towards them that was is like the leaves of the oak
tree and can't be blowed off even by the fiercest
tempests of affliction, still them leaves will wither
in the fall and turn brown and curl up at the
edges, though they don't depart, but stick on tight
as wax all winter until in the spring-time they is
pushed off gently without knowin' it by the green

leaves which come out in real life as well as nater."

When he had finished this opening Mr. Rooper breathed a little sigh of relief. He had not forgotten any of it, and it pleased him.

Marietta sat and looked at him. She had a good sense of humour, and, while she was naturally surprised at what had been said to her, she was greatly amused by it, and really wished to hear what else Thomas Rooper had to say to her.

" Now, madam," he continued, " I am not the man to thrash a tree with a pole to knock the leaves off before their time. But when the young leaves is pushin' and the old leaves is droppin' (not to make any allusion, of course, to any shrivellin' of proper respect), then I come forward, madam, not to take the place of anybody else, but just as the nateral consequence of the seasons, which everybody ought to expect; even such as you, madam, which I may liken to a hemlock - spruce which keeps straight on in the same general line of appearance without no reference to the fall of the year, nor winter, nor summer. And so, Mrs. Himes, I come here to-day to offer to lead you agin to the altar. I have never been there myself, and there ain't no woman in the world that I'd go with but you. I'm a straight-forward person, and when I've got a thing to say, I say it, and now I have said it. And so I set here awaitin' your answer."

At this moment the shutters of the front win-dow, which had been closed, were opened, and Asaph put in his head. "Look here, Thomas Rooper," he said, "these shoes is pegged. I didn't bargain for no pegged shoes ; I wanted 'em sewed ; everything was to be first-class."

Mr. Rooper, who had been leaning forward in his chair, his hands upon his knees, and his face glistening with his expressed feelings as brightly as the old-fashioned but shining silk hat which stood on the floor by his side, turned his head, grew red to the ears, and then sprang to his feet. "Asaph Scantle," he cried, with extended fist, "you have broke your word ; you hindered."

"No, I didn't," said Asaph, sulkily ; "but pegged shoes is too much for any man to stand." And he withdrew from the window, closing the shutters again.

"What does this mean?" asked Mrs. Himes, who had also risen.

"It means," said Thomas, speaking with difficulty, his indignation was so great, "that your brother is a person of tricks and meanders beyond the reach of common human calculation. I don't like to say this of a man who is more or less likely to be my brother-in-law, but I can't help sayin' it, so entirely upset am I at his goin' back on me at such a minute."

"Going back on you?" asked Mrs. Himes. "What do you mean? What has he promised?"

Thomas hesitated. He did not wish to interrupt his courtship by the discussion of any new question, especially this question. "If we could settle what we have been talkin' about, Mrs. Himes," he said, "and if you would give me my answer, then I could git my mind down to commoner things. But swingin' on a hook as I am, I don't know whether my head or my heels is uppermost, or what's revolvin' around me."

"Oh, I can give you your answer quickly enough," she cried. "It is impossible for me to marry you, so that's all settled."

" Impossible is a big word," said Mr. Rooper.
" Has anybody else got afore me ? "

" I am not bound to answer that question," said
Marietta, slightly colouring ; " but I cannot accept
you, Mr. Rooper."

" Then there's somebody else, of course," said
Thomas, gazing darkly upon the floor. " And
what's more, Asaph knew it ; that's just as clear
as daylight. That's what made him come to me
yesterday and go back on his first bargain."

" Now then," said Mrs. Himes, speaking very
decidedly, " I want to know what you mean by
this talk about bargains."

Mr. Rooper knit his brows. " This is mighty
different talk," he said, " from the kind I expected
when I come here. But you have answered
my question, now I'll answer yours. Asaph
Scantle, no longer ago than day before yesterday, after hearin' that things wasn't goin' very
well with me, recommended me to marry you,
and agreed that he would do his level best, by
day and by night, to help me git you, if I would
give him a suit of clothes, an umbrella, and a
dictionary."

At this Mrs. Himes gave a little gasp and sat down.

"Now, I hadn't no thoughts of tradin' for a wife," continued Thomas, "especially in woollen goods and books, but when I considered and turned the matter over in my mind, and thought what a woman you was, and what a life there was afore me if I got you, I agreed to do it. Then he wanted pay aforehand, and that I wouldn't agree to, not because I thought you wasn't wuth it, but because I couldn't trust him if anybody offered him more before I got you. But that ain't the wust of it; yesterday he come down to see me and went back on his bargain, and that, after I I had spent the whole night thinkin' of you and what I was goin' to say. And he put on such high-cockalorum airs that I, bein' as soft as mush around the heart, just wilted and agreed to give him everything he bargained for if he would promise not to hinder. But he wasn't satisfied with that and wouldn't come to no terms until I'd give him my Centennial pipe, what's been like a child to me this many a year. And when he saw how disgruntled I was at sich a loss, he said my pipe might be very dear to me, but his sister was jest as dear to him. And then, on top of the whole thing, he pokes his head through the shutters and hinders jest at the most ticklish moment."

"A dictionary and a pipe!" ejaculated poor Marietta, her eyes fixed upon the floor.

"But I'm goin' to make him give 'em all back," exclaimed Thomas. "They was the price of not hinderin', and he hindered."

"He shall give them back," said Marietta, rising, "but you must understand, Mr. Rooper, that in no way did Asaph interfere with your marrying me. That was a matter with which he did have and could have nothing to do. And now I wish you could get away without speaking to him. I do not want any quarrelling or high words here, and I will see him and arrange the matter better than you can do it."

"Oh, I can git away without speakin' to him," said Mr. Rooper, with reddened face. And so saying, he strode out of the house, through the front yard, and out of the gate without turning his head towards Asaph, still sitting under the tree.

"Oh, ho," said the latter to himself, "she's

II

bounced him short and sharp; and it serves him right, too, after playin' that trick on me. Pegged shoes, indeed!"

At this moment the word "Asaph" came from the house in tones shriller and sharper and higher than any in which he had ever heard it pronounced before. He sprang to his feet and went to the house. His sister took him into the parlour and shut the door. Her eyes were red and her face was pale. "Asaph," said she, "Mr. Rooper has told me the whole of your infamous conduct. Now I know what you meant when you said that you were making arrangements to get clothes. You were going to sell me for them. And when you found out that I was likely to marry Doctor Wicker, you put up your price and wanted a dictionary and a pipe."

"No, Marietta," said Asaph, "the dictionary belonged to the first bargain. If you knew how I need a dictionary——"

"Be still!" she cried. "I do not want you to say a word. You have acted most shamefully toward me, and I want you to go away this very day. And before you go you must give back to

Mr. Rooper everything that you got from him. I
will fit you out with some of Mr. Himes's clothes
and make no conditions at all, only that you shall
go away. Come up stairs with me and I will get
the clothes."

The room in the garret was opened and various
garments which had belonged to the late Mr.
Himes were brought out.

"This is pretty hard on me, Marietta," said
Asaph, as he held up a coat, "to give up new all-
wool goods for things that has been worn and is
part cotton, if I'm a judge."

Marietta said very little. She gave him what
clothes he needed and insisted on his putting them
on, making a package of the things he had received from Mr. Rooper and returning them to
that gentleman. Asaph at first grumbled, but he
finally obeyed with a willingness which might
have excited the suspicions of Marietta had she
not been so angry.

With an enormous package wrapped in brown
paper in one hand and a cane, an umbrella and a
very small hand-bag in the other, Asaph approached the tavern. Mr. Rooper was sitting on

the piazza alone. He was smoking a very common-looking clay pipe and gazing intently into the air in front of him. When his old crony came and stood before the piazza he did not turn his head nor his eyes.

"Thomas Rooper," said Asaph, "you have got me into a very bad scrape. I have been turned out of doors on account of what you said about me. And where I am goin' I don't know, for I can't walk to Drummondville. And what's more, I kept my word and you didn't. I didn't hinder you; for how could I suppose that you was goin' to pop the question the very minute you got inside the door? And that dictionary you promised I've not got."

Thomas Rooper answered not a word, but looked steadily in front of him.

"And there's another thing," said Asaph. "What are you goin' to allow me for that suit of clothes what I've been wearin', what I took off in your room and left there?"

At this Mr. Rooper sprang to his feet with such violence that the fire danced out of the bowl of his pipe. "What is the fare to Drummondville?" he cried.

Asaph reflected a moment. "Three dollars and fifty cents, includin' supper."

"I'll give you that for them clothes," said the other, and counted out the money.

Asaph took it and sighed. "You've been hard on me, Thomas," said he, "but I bear you no grudge. Good-bye."

As he walked slowly towards the station Mr. Scantle stopped at the store. "Has that dictionary come that was ordered for me?" he said; and when told that it could not be expected for several days, he did not despair, for it was possible that Thomas Rooper might be so angry that he would forget to countermand the order; in that case he might yet hope to obtain the coveted book.

The package containing the Rooper winter suit was heavy, and Asaph walked slowly. He did not want to go to Drummondville, for he hated book-keeping, and his year of leisure and good living had spoiled him for work and poor fare. In this moody state he was very glad to stop and have a little chat with Mrs. McJimsey, who was sitting at her front window.

This good lady was the principal dressmaker of the village; and by hard work and attention to business she made a very comfortable living. She was a widow, small of stature, thin of feature, very neatly dressed and pleasant to look at. Asaph entered the little front yard, put his package on the doorstep and stood under the window to talk to her. Dressed in the clothes of the late Mr. Himes, her visitor presented such a respectable appearance that Mrs. McJimsey was not in the least ashamed to have people see him standing there, which she would have been a few days ago. Indeed, she felt complimented that he should want to stop. The conversation soon turned upon her removal from her present abode.

"I'm awfully sorry to have to go," she said; "for my time is up just in the middle of my busy season, and that's goin' to throw me back dreadfully. He hasn't done right by me, that Mr. Rooper, in letting things go to rack and ruin in this way, and me payin' his rent so regular."

"That's true," said Asaph. "Thomas Rooper is a hard man—a hard man, Mrs. McJimsey. I can see how he would be overbearin' with a lone woman like you: neither your son nor your daughter bein' of age yet to take your part."

" Yes, Mr. Scantle, it's very hard."

Asaph stood for a moment looking at a little bed of zinnias by the side of the doorstep. " What you want, Mrs. McJimsey," said he, "is a man in the house."

In an instant Mrs. McJimsey flushed pink. It was such a strange thing for a gentleman to say to her.

Asaph saw the flush. He had not expected that result from his remark, but he was quick to take advantage of it. " Mrs. McJimsey," said he, " you are a widow, and you are imposed upon, and you need somebody to take care of you. If you will put that job into my hands I will do it. I am a man what works with his head, and if you will let me I'll work for you. To put it square, I ask you to marry me. My sister's goin' to be married, and I'm on the pint of goin' away ; for I could not abear to stay in her house when strangers come into it. But if you say the word, I'll stay here and be yours for ever and ever more."

Mrs. McJimsey said not a word, but her head drooped and wild thoughts ran through her brain. Thoughts not wild, but well-trained and broken, ran through Asaph's brain. The idea of going to Drummondville and spending for the journey thither a dollar and seventy-five cents of the money he had received from Mr. Rooper now became absolutely repulsive to him.

"Mrs. McJimsey," said he, "I will say more. Not only do I ask you to marry me, but I ask you to do it now. The evenin' sun is settin', the evenin' birds is singin', and it seems to me, Mrs. McJimsey, that all nater pints to this softenin' hour as a marryin' moment. You say your son won't be home from his work until supper-time, and your daughter has gone out for a walk. Come with me to Mr. Parker's, the Methodist minister, and let us join hands at the altar there. The gardener and his wife is always ready to stand up as witnesses. And when your son and your daughter comes home to supper, they can find their mother here afore 'em married and settled."

"But, Mr. Scantle," exclaimed Mrs. McJimsey, "it's so suddint. What will the neighbours say?"

"As for bein' suddint, Mrs. McJimsey, I've knowed you for nearly a year; and now, bein' on the way to leave what's been my happy home, I couldn't keep the truth from you no longer. And as for the neighbours, they needn't know that we h'ain't been engaged for months."

"It's so queer, so very queer," said the little dressmaker. And her face flushed again, and there were tears, not at all sorrowful ones, in her eyes; and her somewhat needle-pricked right hand accidentally laid itself upon the window sill in easy reach of anyone outside.

The next morning Mr. Rooper, being of a practical way of thinking, turned his thoughts from love and resentment to the subject of his income. And he soon became convinced that it would be better to keep the McJimseys in his house, if it could be done without too great an outlay for repairs. So he walked over to his property. When he reached the house he was almost stupefied to see Asaph in a chair in the front yard, dressed in the new suit of clothes which he, Thomas Rooper, had paid for, and smoking the Centennial pipe.

"Good morning, Mr. Rooper," said Asaph, in a loud and cheery voice. "I suppose you've come to talk to Mrs. McJimsey about the work you've got to do here to make this house fit to live in. But there ain't no Mrs. McJimsey. She's Mrs. Scantle now, and I'm your tenant. You can talk to me."

Doctor Wicker came to see Mrs. Himes in the afternoon of the day he had promised to come, and early in the autumn they were married. Since Asaph Scantle had married and settled he had not seen his sister nor spoken to her; but he determined that on so joyful an occasion as this he would show no resentment. So he attended the wedding in the village church, dressed in the suit of clothes which had belonged to the late Mr. Himes.

A MAN'S birth is generally considered the most important event of his existence, but I truly think that what I am about to relate was more important to me than my entrance into this world ; because, had not these things happened, I am of the opinion that my life would have been of no value to me and my birth a misfortune.

My father, Joshua Cuthbert, died soon after I came to my majority, leaving me what he had considered a comfortable property. This consisted of a large house and some forty acres of land, nearly the whole of which lay upon a bluff, which upon three sides descended to a little valley, through which ran a gentle stream. I had no brothers or sisters. My mother died when I was a boy, and I, Walter Cuthbert, was left the sole representative of my immediate family.

My estate had been a comfortable one to my
father, because his income from the practice of his
profession as a physician enabled him to keep it
up and provide satisfactorily for himself and me.
I had no profession, and but a very small income,
the result of a few investments my father had
made. Left to myself, I felt no inducement to take
up any profession or business. My wants were
simple, and for a few years I lived without ex-
periencing any inconvenience from the economies
which I was obliged to practice. My books, my
dog, my gun, and my rod made life very pleasant
to me, and the subject of an increase of income
never disturbed my mind.

But as time passed on the paternal home began
to present an air of neglect and even dilapidation,
which occasionally attracted my attention and
caused, as I incidentally discovered, a great deal
of unfavourable comment among my neighbours,
who thought that I should go to work and at least
earn money enough to put the house and grounds
in a condition which should not be unworthy the
memory of the good Dr. Cuthbert. In fact, I
began to be looked upon as a shiftless young man;

and, now and then, I found a person old enough and bold enough to tell me so.

But, instead of endeavouring to find some occupation by which I might better my condition and improve my estate, I fell in love, which, in the opinion of my neighbours, was the very worst thing that could have happened to me at this time. I lived in a thrifty region, and for a man who could not support himself to think of taking upon him the support of a wife, especially such a wife as Agnes Havelot would be, was considered more than folly and looked upon as a crime. Everybody knew that I was in love with Miss Havelot, for I went to court her as boldly as I went to fish or shoot. There was a good deal of talk about it, and this finally came to the ears of Mr. Havelot, my lady's father, who, thereupon, promptly ordered her to have no more to do with me.

The Havelot estate, which adjoined mine, was a very large one, containing hundreds and hundreds of acres ; and the Havelots were rich, rich enough to frighten any poor young man of marrying intent. But I did not appreciate the fact that I was a poor young man. I had never troubled my head about money as it regarded myself, and I now did not trouble my head about it as regarded Agnes. I loved her, I hoped she loved me, and all other considerations were thrown aside. Mr. Havelot, however, was a man of a different way of thinking.

It was a little time before I became convinced that the decision of Agnes's father, that there should be no communication between that dear girl and myself, really meant anything. I had never been subjected to restrictions, and I did not understand how people of spirit could submit to them ; but I was made to understand it when Mr. Havelot, finding me wandering about his grounds, very forcibly assured me that if I should make my appearance there again, or if he discovered any attempt on my part to communicate with his daughter in any way, he would send her from home. He concluded the very brief interview by stating that if I had any real regard for his daughter's happiness I would cease attentions which would meet with the most decided disapprobation from her only surviving parent and which would result in exiling her from home. I begged for one more interview with Miss Havelot, and if it had been granted I should have assured her of the state of my affections, no matter if there were reasons to suppose that I would never see her again; but her father very sternly forbade anything of the kind, and I went away crushed.

It was a very hard case, for if I played the part of a bold lover, and tried to see Agnes without regard to the wicked orders of her father, I should certainly be discovered ; and then it would be not only myself, but the poor girl, who would suffer. So I determined that I would submit to the Havelot decree. No matter if I never saw her again never heard the sound of her voice, it would be better to have her near me, to have her breathe the same air, cast up her eyes at the same sky, listen to the same birds, that I breathed, looked at, and listened to, than to have her far away, probably in Kentucky, where I knew she had relatives, and where the grass was blue and the sky probably green, or at any rate would appear so to her if in the least degree she felt as I did in regard to the ties of home and the affinities between the sexes.

I now found myself in a most doleful and even desperate condition of mind. There was nothing in the world which I could have for which I cared. Hunting, fishing, and the rambles through woods and fields that had once been so delightful to me now became tasks which I seldom undertook. The only occupation in which I felt the slightest interest was that of sitting in a tower of my house with a telescope, endeavouring to see my Agnes on some portion of her father's grounds ; but, although I diligently directed my glass at the slightest stretch of lawn or bit of path which I could discern through openings in the foliage, I never caught sight of her. I knew, however, by means of daily questions addressed to my cook, whose daughter was a servant in the Havelot house, that Agnes was yet at home. For that reason I remained at home. Otherwise, I should have become a wanderer.

About a month after I had fallen into this most unhappy state, an old friend came to see me. We had been school-fellows, but he differed from me in almost every respect. He was full of ambition and energy, and, although he was but a few years older than myself, he had already made a name in the world. He was a geologist, earnest and enthusiastic in his studies and his investigations. He told me frankly that the object of his visit was two-fold. In the first place, he wanted to see me, and, secondly, he wanted to make some geological examinations on my grounds, which were situated, as he informed me, upon a terminal moraine, a formation which he had not yet had an opportunity of practically investigating.

I had not known that I lived on a moraine, and now that I knew it, I did not care. But Tom Burton glowed with high spirits and lively zeal as he told me how the great bluff on which my house stood, together with the other hills and wooded terraces which stretched away from it along the side of the valley, had been formed by the minute fragments of rock and soil, which, during ages and ages, had been gradually pushed down from the mountains by a great glacier which once occupied the country to the north-east of my house. "Why, Walter, my boy," he cried, " if I had not read it all in the books I should have known for myself, as soon as I came here, that there had once been a glacier up there, and as it gradually moved to the south-west, it had made this country what it is.

I

Have you a stream down there in that dell which I see lies at right-angles with the valley and opens into it ? "

" No," said I ; " I wish there were one. The only stream we have flows along the valley, and not on my property."

Without waiting for me, Tom ran down into my dell, pushed his way through the underbrush to its upper end, and before long came back flushed with heat and enthusiasm.

" Well, sir," he said, " that dell was once the bed of a glacial stream, and you may as well clear it out and plant corn there if you want to, for there never will be another stream flowing through it until there is another glacier out in the country beyond. And now I want you to let me dig about here. I want to find out what sort of stuff the glacier brought down from the mountains. I will hire a man and will promise you to fill up all the holes I make."

I had no objection to my friend's digging as much as he pleased, and for three days he busied himself in getting samples of the soil of my estate. Sometimes I went out and looked at him, and gradually a little of his earnest ardour infused itself into me, and with some show of interest I looked into the holes he had made and glanced over the mineral specimens he showed me.

"Well, Walter," said he, when he took leave of me, "I am very sorry that I did not discover that the glacier had raked out the bed of a gold-mine from the mountains up there and brought it down to you, or, at any rate, some valuable iron-ore. But I am obliged to say it did not do anything of the sort. But I can tell you one thing it brought you, and, although it is not of any great commercial value, I should think you could make good use of it here on your place. You have one of the finest deposits of gravel on this bluff that I have met with, and if you were to take out a lot of it and spread it over your driveways and paths, it would make it a great deal pleasanter for you to go about here in bad weather, and would wonderfully improve your property. Good roads always give an idea of thrift and prosperity." And then he went away with a valise nearly full of mineral specimens which he assured me were very interesting.

My interest in geological formations died away as soon as Tom Burton had departed, but what he said about making gravel roads, giving the place an air of thrift and prosperity, had its effect upon my mind. It struck me that it would be a very good thing if people in the neighbourhood, especially the Havelots, were to perceive on my place some evidences of thrift and prosperity. Most palpable evidences of unthrift and impecuniosity had cut me off from Agnes, and why might it not be that some signs of improved circumstances would remove, to a degree at least, the restrictions which had been placed between us ? This was but a very little thing upon which to build hopes ; but ever since men and women have loved. they have built grand hopes upon very slight foundations. I determined to put my roadways in order.

My efforts in this direction were really evidence of anything but thriftiness, for I could not in the least afford to make my drives and walks resemble the smooth and beautiful roads which wound over the Havelot estate, although to do this was my intention, and I set about the work without loss of time. I took up this occupation with so much earnestness that it seriously interfered with my observations from the tower.

I hired two men and set them to work to dig a gravel-pit. They made excavations at several places, and very soon found what they declared to be a very fine quality of road-gravel. I ordered them to dig on until they had taken out what they believed to be enough to cover all my roads. When this had been done, I would have it properly spread and rolled. As this promised to be a very good job, the men went to work in fine spirits, and evidently made up their minds that the improvements I desired would require a vast deal of gravel.

When they had dug a hole so deep that it became difficult to throw up the gravel from the bottom, I suggested that they should dig at some other place. But to this they objected, declaring that the gravel was getting better and better, and it would be well to go on down as long as the quality continued to be so good. So, at last, they put a ladder into the pit, one man carrying the gravel up in a hod, while the other dug it ; and

when they had gone down so deep that this was
no longer practicable, they rigged up a derrick and
windlass and drew up the gravel in a bucket.

Had I been of a more practical turn of mind
I might have perceived that this method of working made the job a very long and, consequently,
to the labourers, a profitable one; but no such
idea entered into my head, and not noticing
whether they were bringing up sand or gravel
I allowed them to proceed.

One morning I went out to the spot where
the excavation was being made, and found
that the men had built a fire on the ground near
the opening of the pit, and that one of them was
bending over it warming himself. As the month
was July this naturally surprised me, and I inquired
the reason for so strange a performance.

"Upon my soul," said the man, who was rubbing his hands over the blaze, "I do not wonder
you are surprised; but it is so cold down at the
bottom of that pit that me fingers is almost
frosted; and we haven't struck any wather neither,
which couldn't be expected, of course, a-diggin
down into the hill like this."

I looked into the hole and found it was very deep. " I think it would be better to stop digging here," said I, " and try some other place."

" I wouldn't do that just now," said the other man, who was preparing to go down in the bucket ; " to be sure, it's a good deal more like a well than a gravel-pit, but it's bigger at the top than at the bottom, and there's no danger of it's cavin' in, and now that we've got everything rigged up all right, it would be a pity to make a change yet awhile."

So I let them go on ; but the next day, when I went out again, I found that they had come to the conclusion that it was time to give up digging in that hole. They both declared that it almost froze their feet to stand on the ground where they worked at the bottom of the excavation. The slow business of drawing up the gravel by means of a bucket and windlass was, therefore, reluctantly given up. The men now went to work to dig outward from this pit toward the edge of the bluff which overlooked my little dell, and gradually made a wide trench, which they deepened until— and I am afraid to say how long they worked before this was done — they could walk to the original pit from the level of the dell. They then deepened the inner end of the trench, wheeling out the gravel in barrows, until they had made an inclined pathway from the dell to the bottom of the pit. The wheeling now became difficult, and the men soon declared that they were sure that they had quite gravel enough.

When they made this announcement, and I had gone into some financial calculations, I found that I would be obliged to put an end to my operations, at least for the present, for my available funds were gone, or would be when I had paid what I owed for the work. The men were very much disappointed by the sudden ending of this good job, but they departed, and I was left to gaze upon a vast amount of gravel of which, for the present at least, I could not afford to make the slightest use.

The mental despondency which had been some_ what lightened during my excavating operations now returned, and I became rather more gloomy and downcast than before. My cook declared that it was of no use to prepare meals which I

never ate, and suggested that it would save money
if I discharged her. As I had not paid her anything for a long time, I did not see how this
would benefit me.

Wandering about one day with my hat pulled
down over my eyes, and my hands thrust deep
into my pockets, I strolled into the dell and stood
before the wide trench which led to the pit in
which I had foolishly sunk the money which
should have supported me for months. I entered
this dismal passage and walked slowly and carefully down the incline until I reached the bottom
of the original pit, where I had never been
before. I stood here looking up and around
me, and wondering how men could bring themselves to dig down into such dreary depths simply
for the sake of a few dollars a week, when I involuntarily began to stamp my feet. They were
very cold, although I had not been there more
than a minute. I wondered at this and took up
some of the loose gravel in my hand. It was quite
dry, but it chilled my fingers. I did not understand
it, and did not try to, but walked up the trench
and around into the dell thinking of Agnes.

I was very fond of milk, which, indeed, was almost the only food I now cared for, and I was consequently much disappointed at my noonday meal when I found that the milk had soured and was not fit to drink.

"You see, sir," said Susan, "ice is very scarce and dear, and we cannot afford to buy much of it. There was no freezin' weather last winter, and the price has gone up as high as the thermometer, sir; and so, between the two of 'em, I can't keep things from spoilin'."

The idea now came to me that if Susan would take the milk, and anything else she wished to keep cool in this hot weather, to the bottom of the gravel-pit, she would find the temperature there cold enough to preserve them without ice, and I told her so.

The next morning Susan came to me with a pleased countenance and said, "I put the butter and the milk in that pit last night, and the butter's just as hard and the milk's as hard as if it had been kept in an ice-house. But the place is as cold as an ice-house, sir, and unless I am mistaken, there's ice in it. Anyway, what do you call that?" And she took from a little basket

a piece of greyish ice as large as my fist. "When
I found it was so cold down there, sir," she said,
"I thought I would dig a little myself and see
what made it so; and I took a fire-shovel and
hachet, and, when I had scraped away some of
the gravel, I came to something hard and chopped
off this piece of it, which is real ice sir, or I know
nothing about it. Perhaps there used to be an
ice-house there, and you might get some of it if
you dug, though why anyone should put it down
so deep and then cover it up, I'm sure I don't
know. But as long as there's any there, I think
we should get it out, even if there's only a little
of it; for I cannot take everything down to that
pit, and we might as well have it in the re-
frigerator."

This seemed to me like very good sense, and
if I had had a man I should have ordered him
to go down to the pit and dig up any lumps of
ice he might find and bring them to the house.
But I had no man, and I therefore became impressed with the opinion that if I did not want to
drink sour milk for the rest of the summer, it
might be a good thing for me to go down there
and dig out some of the ice myself. So with

pick-axe and shovel I went to the bottom of the pit and set myself to work.

A few inches below the surface I found that my shovel struck something hard, and, clearing away the gravel from this for two or three square feet, I looked down upon a solid mass of ice. It was dirty and begrimed, but it was truly ice. With my pick I detached some large pieces of it. These, with some discomfort, I carried out into the dell where Susan might come with her basket and get them.

For several days Susan and I took out ice from pit, and then I thought that perhaps Tom Burton might feel some interest in this frozen deposit in my terminal moraine, and so I wrote to him about it. He did not answer my letter, but instead arrived himself the next afternoon.

" Ice at the bottom of a gravel-pit," said he, " is a thing I never heard of. Will you lend me a spade and a pick-axe ? "

When Tom came out of that pit—it was too cold a place for me to go with him and watch his proceedings—I saw him come running towards the house.

" Walter," he shouted, " we must hire all the men we can find and dig, dig, dig. If I am not mistaken, something has happened on your place that is wonderful almost beyond belief. But we must not stop to talk. We must dig, dig, dig; dig all day and dig all night. Don't think of the cost. I'll attend to that. I'll get the money. What we must do is to find men and set them to work."

"What's the matter?" said I. "What has happened?"

"I haven't time to talk about it now! besides, I don't want to, for fear that I should find that I am mistaken. But get on your hat, my dear fellow, and let's go over to the town for men."

The next day there were eight men working under the direction of my friend Burton, and although they did not work at night as he wished them to do, they laboured steadfastly for ten days or more before Tom was ready to announce what it was he had hoped to discover, and whether or not he had found it. For a day or two I watched the workmen from time to time, but after that I kept away, preferring to await the result of my friend's operations. He evidently expected to find something worth having, and whether he was successful or not, it suited me better to know the truth all at once and not by degrees.

On the morning of the eleventh day Tom came into the room where I was reading and sat down near me. His face was pale, his eyes glittering. "Old friend," said he, and as he spoke I noticed that his voice was a little husky, although it was plain enough that his emotion was not occasioned by bad fortune—"my good old friend, I have found out what made the bottom of your gravel-pit so uncomfortably cold. You need not doubt what I am going to tell you, for my excavations have been complete and thorough enough to make me sure of what I say. Don't you remember that I told you that ages ago there was a vast glacier in the country which stretches from here to the mountains? Well, sir, the foot of that glacier must have reached further this way than is generally supposed. At any rate a portion of it did extend in this direction as far as this bit of the world which is now yours. This end, or spur of the glacier, nearly a quarter of a mile in width, I should say, and pushing before it a portion of the terminal moraine on which you live, came slowly toward the valley, until suddenly it detached itself from the main glacier and disappeared from sight. That is to say, my boy "—and as he spoke Tom sprang to his feet, too excited to sit any longer—" it descended to the bowels of the earth, at least for a considerable distance in that direction. Now you want to know how this happened. Well, I'll tell you. In this part of the country there are scattered about here and there great caves. Geologists know one or two of them, and it is certain that there are others undiscovered. Well, sir, your glacier spur discovered one of them, and when it had lain over the top of it for an age or two, and had grown bigger and bigger, and heavier and heavier, it at last burst through the rock roof of the cave, snapping itself from the rest of the glacier and falling in one vast mass to the bottom of the subterranean abyss. Walter, it is there now. The rest of the glacier came steadily down ; the moraines were forced before it ; they covered up this glacier spur, this broken fragment, and by the time the climate changed and the average of temperature rose above that of the glacial period, this vast sunken mass of ice was packed away below the surface of the earth, out of the reach of the action of friction, or heat, or moisture, or anything else which might destroy it. And through all the long procession of centuries that broken end of the glacier has been lying in your terminal moraine. It is there now. It is yours, Walter Cuthbert. It is an ice mine. It is wealth, and so far as I can make out, it is nearly all upon your land. To you is the possession, but to me is the glory of the discovery. A bit of the glacial period kept in a cave for us! It is too wonderful to believe! Walter, have you any brandy?"

It may well be supposed that by this time I was thoroughly awakened to the importance and the amazing character of my friend's discovery, and I hurried with him to the scene of operations. There he explained everything and showed me how, by digging away a portion of the face of the bluff, he had found that this vast fragment of the glacier, which had been so miraculously preserved, ended in an irregularly perpendicular wall, which extended downward he knew not how far, and the edge of it on its upper side had been touched by my work-men in digging their pit. "It was the gradual melting of the upper end of this glacier," said Tom, " probably more elevated than the lower end, that made your dell. I wondered why the depression did not extend further up toward the spot where the foot of the glacier was supposed to have been. This end of the fragment, being sunk in deeper and afterward covered up more completely, probably never melted at all."

" It is amazing—astounding," said I ; " but what of it, now that we have found it ? "

" What of it ? " cried Tom, and his whole form trembled as he spoke. " You have here a source of wealth, of opulence which shall endure for the rest of your days. Here, at your very door, where it can be taken out and transported with the least possible trouble, is ice enough to supply the town, the county, yes, I might say, the State, for hundreds of years. No, sir, I cannot go into supper. I cannot eat. I leave to you the business and practical part of this affair. I go to report upon its scientific features."

" Agnes," I exclaimed, as I walked to the house with my hands clasped and my eyes raised to the sky, " the glacial period has given thee to me ! "

K

This did not immediately follow, although I went that very night to Mr. Havelot and declared to him that I was now rich enough to marry his daughter. He laughed at me in a manner which was very annoying, and made certain remarks which indicated that he thought it probable that it was not the roof of the cave, but my mind, which had given way under the influence of undue pressure.

The contemptuous manner in which I had been received aroused within me a very unusual state of mind. While talking to Mr. Havelot I heard not far away in some part of the house a voice singing. It was the voice of Agnes, and I believed she sang so that I could hear her. But as her sweet tones reached my ear there came to me at the same time the harsh, contemptuous words of her father. I left the house determined to crush that man to the earth beneath a superincumbent mass of ice—or the evidence of the results of the ownership of such a mass—which would make him groan and weep as he apologised to me for his scornful and disrespectful utterances and at the same time offered me the hand of his daughter.

When the discovery of the ice-mine, as it grew

to be called, became generally known, my grounds were crowded by sightseers, and reporters of newspapers were more plentiful than squirrels. But the latter were referred to Burton, who would gladly talk to them as long as they could afford to listen, and I felt myself at last compelled to shut my gates to the first.

I had offers of capital to develop this novel source of wealth, and I accepted enough of this assistance to enable me to begin operations on a moderate scale. It was considered wise not to uncover any portion of the glacier spur, but to construct an inclined shaft down to its wall-like end, and from this tunnel into the great mass. Immediately the leading ice company of the neighbouring town contracted with me for all the ice I could furnish, and the flood-gates of affluence began slowly to rise.

The earliest, and certainly one of the greatest, benefits which came to me from this bequest from the unhistoric past was the new energy and vigour with which my mind and body were now infused. My old, careless method of life and my recent melancholy, despairing mood were gone, and I now began to employ myself upon the main object of my life with an energy and enthusiasm almost equal to that of my friend Tom Burton. This present object of my life was to prepare my home for Agnes.

The great piles of gravel which my men had dug from the well-like pit were spread upon the road-ways and rolled smooth and hard ; my lawn was mowed ; my flower-beds and borders put in order ; useless bushes and undergrowth cut out and cleared away ; my out-buildings were repaired, and grounds around my house rapidly assumed their old ap-pearance of neatness and beauty.

Ice was very scarce that summer, and, as the waggons wound away from the opening of the shaft which led down to the glacier, carrying their loads to the nearest railway station, so money came to me ; not in large sums at first, for preparations had not yet been perfected for taking out the ice in great quantities, but enough to enable me to go on with my work as rapidly as I could plan it. I set about renovating and brightening and newly fur-nishing my house. Whatever I thought that Agnes would like I bought and put into it. I tried to put myself in her place as I selected the paper-hangings and the materials with which to cover the furniture.

Sometimes, while thus employed selecting ornaments or useful articles for my house, and using as far as was possible the taste and judgment of another instead of my own, the idea came to me that perhaps Agnes had never heard of my miraculous good fortune. Certainly her father would not be likely to inform her, and perhaps she still thought of me, if she thought at all, as the poor young man from whom she had been obliged to part because he was poor.

But whether she knew that I was growing rich, or whether she thought I was becoming poorer and poorer, I thought only of the day when I could go to her father and tell him that I was able to take his daughter and place her in a home as beautiful as that in which she now lived, and maintain her with all the comforts and luxuries which he could give her.

One day I asked my faithful cook, who also acted as my housekeeper and general supervisor, to assist me in making out a list of china which I intended to purchase.

"Are you thinking of buying china, sir?" she asked. "We have now quite as much as we really need."

"Oh, yes," said I, "I shall get complete sets of everything than can be required for a properly furnished household."

Susan gave a little sigh. "You are spendin' a lot of money, sir, and some of it for things that a single gentleman would not be likely to care very much about; and if you was to take it into your head to travel and stay away for a year or two, there's a good many things you've bought that would look shabby when you come back, no matter how careful I might be in dustin' 'em and keepin' 'em covered."

"But I have no idea of travelling," said I. "There's no place so pleasant as this to me."

Susan was silent for a few moments, and then she said: "I know very well why you are doing this, and I feel it my bounden duty to say to you that there's a chance of it's being no use. I do not speak without good reason, and I would not do it if I didn't think that it might make trouble lighter to you when it comes."

" What are you talking about, Susan ? What do you mean ? "

" Well, sir, this is what I mean : It was only last night that my daughter Jane was in Mr. Havelot's dining-room after dinner was over, and Mr. Have-lot and a friend of his were sitting there, smoking their cigars and drinking their coffee. She went in and came out again as she was busy takin' away the dishes, and they paid no attention to her, but went on talkin' without knowin', most likely, she was there. Mr. Havelot and the gentleman were talking about you, and Jane she heard Mr. Havelot say as plain as anything, and she said she couldn't be mistaken, that even if your nonsensical ice-mine proved to be worth anything, he would never let his daughter marry an iceman. He spoke most disrespectfully of icemen, sir, and said that it would make him sick to have a son-in-law whose business it was to sell ice to butchers, and hotels, and grog-shops, and pork-packers, and all that sort of people ; and that he would as soon have his daughter marry the man who supplied a hotel with sausages as the one who supplied it with ice to keep those sausages from spoiling. You see, sir, Mr. Havelot lives on

his property as his father did before him, and he is
a very proud man, with a heart as hard and cold as
that ice down under your land ; and it's borne in
on me very strong, sir, that it would be a bad thing
for you to keep on thinkin' that you are getting
this house all ready to bring Miss Havelot to when
you have married her.   For if Mr. Havelot keeps
on livin', which there's every chance of his doin', it
may be many a weary year before you get Miss
Agnes, if ever you get her.   And havin' said that,
sir, I say no more, and I would not have said this
much if I hadn't felt it my bounden duty to your
father's son to warn him that most likely he was
workin' for what he might never get, and so keep
him from breakin' his heart when he found out the
truth all of a sudden."

With that Susan left me, without offering any
assistance in making out a list of china.   This was
a terrible story ; but, after all, it was founded only
upon servants' gossip.   In this country even proud,
rich men like Mr. Havelot did not have such absurd
ideas regarding the source of wealth.   Money is
money, and whether it be derived from the ordinary products of the earth, from which came much

of Mr. Havelot's revenue, or from an extraordinary
project such as my glacier spur, it truly could not
matter so far as concerned the standing in society
of its possessor. What utter absurdity was this
which Susan had told me! If I were to go to Mr.
Havelot and tell him that I would not marry his
daughter because he supplied brewers and bakers
with the products of his fields, would he not consider me an idiot? I determined to pay no attention to the idle tale. But, alas! determinations of
that sort are often of little avail. I did pay attention to it, and my spirits drooped.

The tunnel into the glacier spur had now attained
considerable length, and the ice in the interior
was found to be of much finer quality than
that first met with, which was of a greyish
hue and somewhat inclined to crumble. When
the workmen reached a grade of ice as good
as they could expect, they began to enlarge the
tunnel into a chamber, and from this they proposed
to extend tunnels in various directions after the
fashion of a coal-mine. The ice was hauled out on
sledges through the tunnel and then carried up a
wooden railway to the mouth of the shaft.

It was comparatively easy to walk down the shaft and enter the tunnel, and when it happened that the men were not at work I allowed visitors to go down and view this wonderful ice-cavern. The walls of the chamber appeared semi-transparent, and the light of candles or lanterns gave the whole scene a weird and beautiful aspect. It was almost possible to imagine oneself surrounded by limpid waters, which might at any moment rush upon him and engulf him.

Every day or two Tom Burton came with a party of scientific visitors, and had I chosen to stop the work of taking out ice, admitted the public and charged a price for admission, I might have made almost as much money as I at that time derived from the sale of the ice. But such a method of profit was repugnant to me.

For several days after Susan's communication to me I worked on in my various operations, endeavouring to banish from my mind the idle nonsense she had spoken of; but one of its effects upon me was to make me feel that I ought not to allow hopes so important to rest upon uncertainties. So I determined that as soon as my house and grounds should be in a condition with which I should for the time be satisfied, I would go boldly to Mr. Havelot, and, casting out of my recollection everything that Susan had said, invite him to visit me and see for himself the results of the discovery of which he had spoken with such derisive contempt. This would be a straightforward and business-like answer to his foolish objections to me, and I believed that in his heart the old gentleman would properly appreciate my action.

About this time there came to my place Aaron Boyce, an elderly farmer of the neighbourhood, and, finding me outside, he seized the opportunity to have a chat with me.

"I tell you what it is, Mr. Cuthbert," said he, "the people in this neighbourhood hasn't give you credit for what's in you. The way you have fixed up this place, and the short time you have took to do it, is enough to show us now what sort of a man you are; and I tell you, sir, we're proud of you for a neighbour. I don't believe there's another gentleman in this county of your age that could have done what you have done in so short a time. I expect now you will be thinking of getting married and startin' housekeepin' in a regular fashion. That comes just as natural as to set hens in the spring. By the way, have you heard that old Mr. Havelot's thinkin' of goin' abroad? I didn't believe he would ever do that again, because he's gettin' pretty well on in years, but old men will do queer things as well as young ones."

" Going abroad ! " I cried. " Does he intend to take his daughter with him ? "

Mr. Aaron Boyce smiled grimly. He was a great old gossip, and he had already obtained the information he wanted. " Yes," he said, " I've heard it was on her account he's going. She's been kind of weakly lately, they tell me, and hasn't took to her food, and the doctors has said that what she wants is a sea-voyage and a change to foreign parts."

Going abroad ! Foreign parts ! This was more terrible than anything I had imagined. I would go to Mr. Havelot that very evening, the only time which I would be certain to find him at home, and talk to him in a way which would be sure to bring him to his senses, if he had any. And if I should find that he had no sense of

propriety or justice, no sense of his duty to his
fellow-man and to his offspring, then I would
begin a bold fight for Agnes, a fight which I would
not give up until, with her own lips, she told me
that it would be useless. I would follow her to
Kentucky, to Europe, to the uttermost ends of the
earth. I could do it now. The frozen deposits in
my terminal moraine would furnish me with the
means. I walked away and left the old farmer
standing grinning. No doubt my improvements
and renovations had been the subject of gossip in
the neighbourhood, and he had come over to see
if he could find out anything definite in regard to
the object of them. He had succeeded, but he
had done more ; he had nerved me to instantly
begin the conquest of Agnes, whether by diplo-
macy or war.

I was so anxious to begin this conquest that I
could scarcely wait for the evening to come. At
the noon-hour, when the ice-works were deserted,
I walked down the shaft and into the ice-chamber
to see what had been done since my last visit. I
decided to insist that operations upon a larger
scale should be immediately begun, in order that I

might have plenty of money with which to carry on my contemplated campaign. Whether it was one of peace or war, I should want all the money I could get.

I took with me a lantern and went round the chamber, which was now twenty-five or thirty feet in diameter, examining the new inroads which had been made upon its walls. There was a tunnel commenced opposite the one by which the chamber was entered, but it had not been opened more than a dozen feet, and it seemed to me that the men had not been working with any very great energy. I wanted to see a continuous stream of ice-blocks from that chamber to the mouth of the shaft.

While grumbling thus I heard behind me a sudden noise like thunder and the crashing of walls, and, turning quickly, I saw that a portion of the roof of the chamber had fallen in. Nor had it ceased to fall. As I gazed, several great masses of ice came down from above and piled themselves upon that which had already fallen.

Startled and frightened, I sprang toward the opening of the entrance tunnel; but, alas! I found that that was the point where the roof had given way, and between me and the outer world was a wall of solid ice, through which it would be as impossible for me to break as if it were a barrier of rock. With the quick instinct which comes to men in danger, I glanced about to see if the workmen had left their tools; but there were none. They had been taken outside. Then I stood and gazed stupidly at the mass of fallen ice, which, even as I looked upon it, was cracking and snapping, pressed down by the weight above it, and forming itself into an impervious barrier without crevice or open seam.

Then I madly shouted. But of what avail were shouts down there in the depths of the earth? I soon ceased this useless expenditure of strength, and, with my lantern in my hand, began to walk around the chamber, throwing the light upon the walls and the roof. I became impressed with the fear that the whole cavity might cave in at once and bury me here in a tomb of ice. But I saw no cracks, nor any sign of further disaster. But why think of anything more? Was not this enough? For, before that ice-barrier could be cleared away, would I not freeze to death?

I now continued to walk, not because I expected

to find anything or do anything, but simply to keep myself warm by action. As long as I could move about I believed that there was no immediate danger of succumbing to the intense cold; for, when a young man, travelling in Switzerland, I had been in the cave of a glacier, and it was not cold enough to prevent some old women from sitting there to play the zither for the sake of a few coppers from visitors. I could not expect to be able to continue walking until I should be rescued, and if I sat down, or by chance slept from exhaustion, I must perish.

The more I thought of it, the more sure I became that in any case I must perish. A man in a block of ice could have no chance of life. And Agnes! Oh, heavens! what demon of the ice had leagued with old Havelot to shut me up in this frozen prison? For a long time I continued to walk, beat my body with my arms, and stamp my feet. The instinct of life was strong within me. I would live as long as I could, and think of Agnes. When I should be frozen I could not think of her.

Sometimes I stopped and listened. I was sure

I could hear noises, but I could not tell whether they were above me or not. In the centre of the ice-barrier, about four feet from the ground, was a vast block of the frozen substance which was unusually clear and seemed to have nothing on the other side of it ; for through it I could see flickers of light, as though people were going about with lanterns. It was quite certain that the accident had been discovered, for, had not the thundering noise been heard by persons outside, the workmen would have seen what had happened as soon as they came into the tunnel to begin their afternoon operations.

At first I wondered why they did not set to work with a will and cut away this barrier and let me out. But there suddenly came to my mind a reason for this lack of energy which was more chilling than the glistening walls around me : Why should they suppose that I was in the ice-chamber ? I was not in the habit of coming here very often, but I was in the habit of wandering off by myself at all hours of the day. This thought made me feel that I might as well lie down on the floor of this awful cave and die at once. The

L

workmen might think it unsafe to mine any further in this part of the glacier, and begin operations at some other point. I did sit down for a moment, and then I rose involuntarily and began my weary round. Suddenly I thought of looking at my watch. It was nearly five o'clock. I had been more than four hours in that dreadful place, and I did not believe that I could continue to exercise my limbs very much longer. The lights I had seen had ceased. It was quite plain that the workmen had no idea that anyone was imprisoned in the cave.

But soon after I had come to this conclusion I saw through the clear block of ice a speck of light, and it became stronger and stronger, until I believed it to be close to the other side of the block. There it remained stationary; but there seemed to be other points of light which moved about in a strange way, and near it. Now I stood by the block watching. When my feet became very cold I stamped them; but there I stood fascinated, for what I saw was truly surprising. A large coal of fire appeared on the other side of the block; then it suddenly vanished and was succeeded by another coal. This disappeared, and another took its place, each one seeming to come nearer and nearer to me. Again and again did these coals appear. They reached the centre of the block ; they approached my side of it. At last one was so near to me that I thought it was about to break through, but it vanished. Then there came a few quick thuds and the end of a piece of iron protruded from the block. This was withdrawn, and through the aperture there came a voice, which said, " Mr. Cuthbert, are you in there?" It was the voice of Agnes !

Weak and cold as I was, fire and energy rushed through me at these words. "Yes," I exclaimed, my mouth to the hole ; "Agnes, is that you ?"

"Wait a minute," came from the other side of the aperture. " I must make it bigger. I must keep it from closing up."

Again came the coals of fire, running backward and forward through the long hole in the block of ice. I could see now what they were. They were irons used by plumbers for melting solder and that sort of thing, and Agnes was probably heating them in a little furnace outside, and withdrawing them as fast as they cooled. It was not long before the aperture was very much enlarged; and then there came grating through it a long tin tube nearly two inches in diameter, which almost, but not quite, reached my side of the block.

Now came again the voice of Agnes: "Oh, Mr. Cuthbert, are you truly there? Are you crushed? Are you wounded? Are you nearly frozen? Are you starved? Tell me quickly if you are yet safe."

Had I stood in a palace padded with the softest silk and filled with spicy odours from a thousand rose-gardens, I could not have been better satisfied with my surroundings than I was at that moment. Agnes was not two feet away! She was telling me that she cared for me! In a very few words I assured her that I was uninjured. Then I was on the point of telling her I loved her, for I believed that not a moment should be lost in making this avowal. I could not die without her knowing that. But the appearance of a mass of paper at the other end of the tube prevented the expression of my sentiments. This was slowly pushed on until I could reach it. Then there came the words:

"Mr. Cuthbert, these are sandwiches. Eat them immediately and walk about while you are doing it. You must keep yourself warm until the men get to you."

Obedient to the slightest wish of this dear creature, I went twice round the cave, devouring the sandwiches as I walked. They were the most delicious food that I had ever tasted. They were given to me by Agnes. I came back to the opening. I could not immediately begin my avowal. I must ask a question first. "Can they get to me?" I inquired. " Is anybody trying to do that? Are they working there by you? I do not hear them at all."

"Oh, no," she answered ; "they are not working here. They are on top of the bluff, trying to dig down to you. They were afraid to meddle with the ice here for fear that more of it might come down and crush you and the men, too. Oh, there has been dreadful excitement since it was found that you were in there!"

" How could they know I was here?" I asked.

" It was your old Susan who first thought of it. She saw you walking towards the shaft about

noon, and then she remembered that she had not
seen you again; and when they came into the
tunnel here they found one of the lanterns gone
and the big stick you generally carry lying where
the lantern had been. Then it was known that
you must be inside. Oh, then there was an awful
time! The foreman of the icemen examined
everything, and said they must dig down to you
from above. He put his men to work; but they
could do very little, for they had hardly any
spades. Then they sent into town for help, and
over to the new park for the Italians working
there. From the way these men set to work you
might have thought that they would dig away the
whole bluff in about five minutes; but they didn't.
Nobody seemed to know what to do, or how to get
to work; and the hole they made when they did
begin was filled up with men almost as fast as they
threw out the stones and gravel. I don't believe
anything would have been done properly if your
friend, Mr. Burton, hadn't happened to come with
two scientific gentlemen, and since that he has
been directing everything. You can't think what
a splendid fellow he is! I fairly adored him when

I saw him giving his orders and making everybody skip around in the right way."

"Tom is a very good man," said I ; "but it is his business to direct that sort of work, and it is not surprising that he knows how to do it. But, Agnes, they may never get down to me, and we do not know that this roof may not cave in upon me at any moment ; and before this or anything else happens I want to tell you——"

"Mr. Cuthbert," said Agnes, "is there plenty of oil in your lantern ? It would be dreadful if it were to go out and leave you there in the dark. I thought of that and brought you a little bottle of kerosene so that you can fill it. I am going to push the bottle through now, if you please." And with this a large phial, cork-end foremost, came slowly through the tube, propelled by one of the soldering-irons. Then came Agnes's voice: "Please fill your lantern immediately, because if it goes out you cannot find it in the dark ; and then walk several times around the cave, for you have been standing still too long already."

I obeyed these injunctions, but in two or three minutes was again at the end of the tube. "Agnes," said I, "how did you happen to come here? Did you contrive in your own mind this method of communicating with me?"

"Oh, yes; I did," she said. ."Everybody said that this mass of ice must not be meddled with, but I knew very well it would not hurt it to make a hole through it."

"But how did you happen to be here?" I asked.

"Oh, I ran over as soon as I heard of the accident. Everybody ran here. The whole neighbourhood is on top of the bluff; but nobody wanted to come into the tunnel, because they were afraid that more of it might fall in. So I was able to work here all by myself, and I am very glad of it. I saw the soldering-iron and the little furnace outside of your house where the plumbers had been using them, and I brought them here myself. Then I thought that a simple hole through the ice might soon freeze up again, and if you were alive inside I could not do anything to help you; and so I ran home and got my diploma-case, that had had one end melted out of it, and I brought that to stick in the hole. I'm so glad that it is long enough, or almost."

"Oh, Agnes," I cried, "you thought of all this for me?"

"Why, of course, Mr. Cuthbert," she answered, before I had a chance to say anything more. "You were in great danger of perishing before the men got to you, and nobody seemed to think of any way to give you immediate relief. And don't you think that a collegiate education is a good thing for girls— at least, that it was for me."

"Agnes," I exclaimed, "please let me speak. I want to tell you, I must tell you——"

But the voice of Agnes was clearer than mine, and it overpowered my words. "Mr. Cuthbert," she said, "we cannot both speak through this tube at the same time in opposite directions. I have here a bottle of water for you, but I am very much afraid it will not go through the diploma-case."

"Oh, I don't want any water," I said. "I can eat ice if I am thirsty. What I want is to tell you——"

"Mr. Cuthbert," said she, "you must not eat that ice. Water that was frozen countless ages ago may be very different from the water of modern times, and might not agree with you. Don't touch it, please. I am going to push the bottle through if I can. I tried to think of everything that you might need, and brought them all at once; because if I could not keep the hole open, I wanted to get them to you without losing a minute."

Now the bottle came slowly through. It was a small beer bottle, I think, and several times I was afraid it was going to stick fast and cut off communication between me and the outer world; that is to say, between me and Agnes. But at last the cork and the neck appeared, and I pulled it through. I did not drink any of it, but immediately applied my mouth to the tube.

" Agnes," I said, "my dear Agnes, you really must not prevent me from speaking. I cannot delay another minute. This is an awful position for me to be in, and as you don't seem to realise——"

" But I do realise, Mr. Cuthbert, that if you don't walk about you will certainly freeze before you can be rescued. Between every two or three words you want to take at least one turn around that place. How dreadful it would be if you were suddenly to become benumbed and stiff! Everybody is thinking of that. The best diggers that Mr. Burton had were three coloured men ; but after they had gone down nothing like as deep as a well, they came up frightened, and said they would not dig another shovelful for the whole world. Perhaps you don't know it, but there's a story about the neighbourhood that the negro hell is under your property. You know many of the coloured people expect to be everlastingly punished with ice and not with fire——"

" Agnes," I interrupted, " I am punished with ice and fire both. Please let me tell you——"

" I was going on to say, Mr. Cuthbert," she interrupted, " that when the Italians heard why the coloured men had come out of the hole they would not go in either, for they are just as afraid of ever-lasting ice as the negroes are, and were sure that if the bottom came out of that hole they would fall into a frozen lower world. So there was nothing to do but to send for paupers, and they are working now. You know paupers have to do what they are told without regard to their beliefs. They got a dozen of them from the poorhouse. Somebody said they just threw them into the hole. Now I must stop talking, for it is time for you to walk around again. Would you like another sandwich?"

"Agnes," said I, endeavouring to speak calmly, "all I want is to be able to tell you——"

"And when you walk, Mr. Cuthbert, you had better keep around the edge of the chamber, for there is no knowing when they may come through. Mr. Burton and the foreman of the icemen measured the bluff so that they say the hole they are making is exactly over the middle of the chamber you are in, and if you walk around the edge the pieces may not fall on you."

"If you don't listen to me, Agnes," I said, "I'll go and sit anywhere, everywhere, where death may come to me quickest. Your coldness is worse than the coldness of the cave. I cannot bear it."

"But, Mr. Cuthbert," said Agnes, speaking, I thought, with some agitation, "I have been listening to you, and what more can you possibly have to say? If there is anything you want, let me know. I will run and get it for you."

"There is no need that you should go away to

get what I want," I said. "It is there with you. It is you."

"Mr. Cuthbert," said Agnes, in a very low voice, but so distinctly that I could hear every word, "don't you think it would be better for you to give your whole mind to keeping yourself warm and strong? For if you let yourself get benumbed you may sink down and freeze."

"Agnes," I said, "I will not move from this little hole until I have told you that I love you, that I have no reason to care for life or rescue unless you return my love, unless you are willing to be mine. Speak quickly to me, Agnes, because I may not be rescued, and may never know whether my love for you is returned or not."

At this moment there was a tremendous crash behind me, and, turning, I saw a mass of broken ice upon the floor of the cave, with a cloud of dust and smaller fragments still falling. And then with a great scratching and scraping, and a howl loud enough to waken the echoes of all the lower regions, down came a red-headed drunken shoe-maker. I cannot say that he was drunk at that moment, but I knew the man the moment I saw his carroty poll, and it was drink which had sent him to the poor-house.

But the sprawling and howling cobbler did not reach the floor. A rope had been fastened around his waist to prevent a fall in case the bottom of the pit should suddenly give way, and he hung dangling in mid-air with white face and distended eyes, cursing and swearing and vociferously entreating to be pulled up. But before he received any answer from above, or I could speak to him, there came through the hole in the roof of the cave a shower of stones and gravel, and with them a frantic Italian, his legs and arms outspread, his face wild with terror.

Just as he appeared in view he grasped the rope of the cobbler, and, though in a moment he came down heavily upon the floor of the chamber, this broke his fall, and he did not appear to be hurt. Instantly he crouched low and almost upon all fours, and began to run around the chamber, keeping close to the walls and screaming, I suppose to preserve him from the torments of the frozen damned.

In the midst of this hubbub came the voice of

Agnes through the hole : "Oh, Mr. Cuthbert, what has happened? Are you alive?"

I was so disappointed by the appearance of these wretched interlopers at the moment it was about to be decided whether my life—should it last for years, or but for a few minutes—was to be black or bright, and I was so shaken and startled by the manner of their entry upon the scene, that I could not immediately shape the words necessary to inform Agnes what had happened. But, collecting my faculties, I was about to speak, when suddenly, with the force of the hind leg of a mule, I was pushed away from the aperture, and the demoniac Italian clapped his great mouth to the end of the tube and roared through it a volume of oaths and supplications. I attempted to thrust aside the wretched being, but I might as well have tried to move the ice barrier itself. He had perceived that someone outside was talking to me, and in his frenzy he was imploring that someone should let him out.

While still endeavouring to move the man, I was seized by the arm, and turning, beheld the pallid face of the shoemaker. They had let him down so that he reached the floor. He tried to fall on his knees before me, but the rope was so short that he was able to go only part of the way down, and presented a most ludicrous appearance, with his toes scraping the icy floor and his arms thrown out as if he were paddling like a tadpole. "Oh, have mercy upon me, sir," he said, "and help me get out of this dreadful place. If you go to the hole and call up it's you, they will pull me up; but if they get you out first they will never think of me. I am a poor pauper, sir, but I never did nothin' to be packed in ice before I am dead."

Noticing that the Italian had left the end of the aperture in the block of ice, and that he was now shouting up the open shaft, I ran to the channel of communication which my Agnes had opened for me, and called through it; but the dear girl had gone.

The end of a ladder now appeared at the opening in the roof; and this was let down until it reached the floor. I started toward it, but before I had gone half the distance the frightened shoe-maker and the maniac Italian sprang upon it, and, with shrieks and oaths, began a maddening fight for possession of the ladder. They might quickly have gone up one after the other, but each had no thought but to be first; and as one seized the rounds he was pulled away by the other, until I feared the ladder would be torn to pieces. The shoemaker finally pushed his way up a little distance, when the Italian sprang upon his back, endeavouring to climb over him; and so on they went up the shaft, fighting, swearing, kicking, scratching, shaking and wrenching the ladder, which had been tied to another one in order to increase its length, so that it was in danger of breaking, and tearing at each other in a fashion which made it wonderful that they did not both tumble headlong downward. They went on up, so completely filling the shaft with their struggling forms and their wild cries that I could not see or hear anything, and was afraid, in fact, to look up toward the outer air.

As I was afterward informed, the Italian, who had slipped into the hole by accident, ran away like a frightened hare the moment he got his feet on firm ground, and the shoemaker sat down and

M

swooned. By this performance he obtained from a benevolent bystander a drink of whisky, the first he had had since he was committed to the poorhouse.

But a voice soon came down the shaft calling to me. I recognised it as that of Tom Burton, and replied that I was safe, and that I was coming up the ladder. But in my attempt to climb, I found that I was unable to do so. Chilled and stiffened by the cold and weakened by fatigue and excitement, I believe I never should have been able to leave that ice-chamber if my faithful friend had not come down the ladder and vigorously assisted me to reach the outer air.

Seated on the ground, my back against a great oak-tree, I was quickly surrounded by a crowd of my neighbours, the workmen and the people who had been drawn to the spot by the news of the strange accident to gaze at me as if I were some unknown being excavated from the bowels of the earth. I was sipping some brandy-and-water which Burton had handed me, when Aaron Boyce pushed himself in front of me.

"Well, sir," he said, "I am mighty glad you got

out of that scrape. I'm bound to say I didn't expect you would. I have been sure all along that it wasn't right to meddle with things that go agin Nature, and I haven't any doubt that you'll see that for yourself and fill up all them tunnels and shafts you've made. The ice that comes on ponds and rivers was good enough for our fore-fathers, and it ought to be good enough for us. And as for this cold stuff you find in your gravel pit, I don't believe it's ice at all; and if it is, like as not it's made of some sort of pizen stuff that freezes easier than water. For everybody knows that water don't freeze in a well, and if it don't do that, why should it do it in any kind of a hole in the ground? So perhaps its just as well that you did git shut up there, sir, and find out for yourself what a dangerous thing it is to fool with Nature and try to get ice from the bottom of the ground instead of the top of the water."

This speech made me angry, for I knew that old Boyce was a man who was always glad to get hold of anything which had gone wrong and to try to make it worse; but I was too weak to answer him.

M 2

This, however, would not have been necessary, for Tom Burton turned upon him. "Idiot," said he, "if that is your way of thinking, you might as well say that if a well caves in you should never again dig for water, or that nobody should have a cellar under his house for fear that the house should fall into it. There's no more danger of the ice beneath us ever giving way again than there is that this bluff should crumble under our feet. That break in the roof of the ice-tunnel was caused by my digging away the face of the bluff very near that spot. The high temperature of the outer air weakened the ice, and it fell. But down here, under this ground and secure from the influences of the heat of the outer air, the mass of ice is more solid than rock. We will build a brick arch over the place where the accident happened, and then there will not be a safer mine on this continent than this ice-mine will be."

This was a wise and diplomatic speech from Burton, and it proved to be of great service to me; for the men who had been taking out ice had been a good deal frightened by the fall of the tunnel, and when it was proved that what Burton had said in regard to the cause of the weakening of the ice was entirely correct, they became willing to go to work again.

I now began to feel stronger and better, and, rising to my feet, I glanced here and there into the crowd, hoping to catch a sight of Agnes. But I was not very much surprised at not seeing her, because she would naturally shrink from forcing herself into the midst of this motley company; but I felt that I must go and look for her without the loss of a minute, for if she should return to her father's house I might not be able to see her again.

On the outskirts of the crowd I met Susan, who was almost overpowered with joy at seeing me safe again. I shook her by the hand, but, without replying to her warm-hearted protestations of thankfulness and delight, I asked her if she had seen Miss Havelot.

"Miss Agnes!" she exclaimed. "Why, no, sir; I expect she's at home; and if she did come here with the rest of the neighbours I didn't see her; for when I found out what had happened, sir, I was so weak that I sat down in the kitchen all of a lump, and have just had strength enough to come out."

"Oh, I know she was here," I cried; "I am sure of that, and I do hope she's not gone home again."

"Know she was here!" exclaimed Susan. "Why, how on earth could you know that?"

I did not reply that it was not on the earth but under it that I became aware of the fact, but hurried toward the Havelot house, hoping to overtake Agnes if she had gone that way. But I did not see her, and suddenly a startling idea struck me, and I turned and ran home as fast as I could go. When I reached my grounds I went directly to the mouth of the shaft. There was nobody there, for the crowd was collected into a solid mass on the top of the bluff, listening to a lecture from Tom Burton, who deemed it well to promote the growth of interest and healthy opinion in regard to his wonderful discovery and my valuable possession. I hurried down the shaft, and near the end of it, just before it joined the ice-tunnel, I beheld Agnes sitting upon the wooden track. She was not unconscious, for as I approached she slightly turned her head. I sprang toward her; I kneeled beside her; I took her in my arms. "Oh, Agnes, dearest Agnes," I cried, "what is the matter? What has happened to you? Has a piece of ice fallen upon you? Have you slipped and hurt yourself?"

She turned her beautiful eyes up toward me and for a moment did not speak. Then she said: "And they got you out? And you are in your right mind?"

"Right mind!" I exclaimed. "I have never been out of my mind. What are you thinking of?"

"Oh, you must have been," she said, "when you screamed at me in that horrible way. I was so frightened that I fell back, and I must have fainted."

Tremulous as I was with love and anxiety, I could not help laughing. "Oh, my dear Agnes, I did not scream at you. That was a crazed Italian who fell through the hole that they dug." Then I told her what had happened.

She heaved a gentle sigh. "I am so glad to hear that," she said. "There was one thing that I was thinking about just before you came and which gave me a little bit of comfort: the words and yells I heard were dreadfully oniony, and somehow or other I could not connect that sort of thing with you."

It now struck me that during this conversation I

had been holding my dear girl in my arms, and she had not shown the slightest sign of resistance or disapprobation. This made my heart beat high. "Oh, Agnes," I said, "I truly believe you love me, or you would not have been here, you would not have done for me all that you did. Why did you not answer me when I spoke to you through that wall of ice, through the hole your dear love had made in it? Why, when I was in such a terrible situation, not knowing whether I was to die or live, did you not comfort my heart with one sweet word?"

"Oh, Walter," she answered, "it wasn't at all necessary for you to say all that you did say, for I had suspected it before, and as soon as you began to call me Agnes I knew, of course, how you felt about it. And, besides, it really was necessary that you should move about to keep yourself from freezing. But the great reason for my not encouraging you to go on talking in that way was that I was afraid people might come into the tunnel, and as, of course, you would not know that they were there, you would go on making love to me through my diploma-case, and you know I should have perished with shame if I had had to stand there with that old Mr. Boyce, and I don't know who else, listening to your words, which were very sweet to me, Walter, but which would have sounded awfully funny to them."

When she said that my words had been sweet to her I dropped the consideration of all other subjects.

When, about ten minutes afterward, we came out of the shaft we were met by Susan.

"Bless my soul and body, Mr. Cuthbert!" she exclaimed. "Did you find that young lady down there in the centre of the earth? It seems to me as if everything that you want comes to you out of the ground. But I have been looking for you to tell you that Mr. Havelot has been here after his daughter, and I'm sure if he had known where she was, he would have been scared out of his wits."

"Father here!" exclaimed Agnes. "Where is he now?"

"I think he has gone home, miss. Indeed, I'm sure of it; for my daughter Jennie, who was over here the same as all the other people in the county, I truly believe told him—and I was proud she had the spirit to speak up that way to him—that your heart was almost broke when you heard about Mr. Cuthbert being shut up in the ice, and that most likely you was in your own room a-cryin' your eyes out. When he heard that he stood lookin' all around the place, and then he asked me if he might go in the house ; and when I told him he was most welcome, he went in. I offered to show him about, which he said was no use, that he had been there often enough ; and he went everywhere, I truly believe, except in the garret and the cellar. And after he got through with that he went out to the barn and then walked home."

" I must go to him immediately," said Agnes.

" But not alone," said I. And together we walked through the woods, over the little field and across the Havelot lawn to the house. We were told the old gentleman was in his library, and together we entered the room.

Mr. Havelot was sitting by a table on which were lying several open volumes of an encyclopædia. When he turned and saw us, he closed his book, pushed back his chair, and took off his spectacles. " Upon my word, sir," he cried ; " and so the first thing you do after they pull you out of the earth is to come here and break my commands."

"I came on the invitation of your daughter, sir."

"And what right has she to invite you, I'd like to know?"

"She has every right, for to her I owe my existence."

"What rabid nonsense!" exclaimed the old gentleman. "People don't owe their existence to the silly creatures they fall in love with."

"I assure you I am correct, sir." And then I related to him what his daughter had done, and how through her angelic agency my rescuers had found me a living being instead of a frozen corpse.

"Stuff!" said Mr. Havelot. "People can live in a temperature of thirty-two degrees above zero all winter. Out in Minnesota they think that's hot. And you gave him victuals and drink through your diploma-case! Well, miss, I told you that if you tried to roast chestnuts in that diploma-case the bottom would come out."

"But you see, father," said Agnes, earnestly, "the reason I did that was because when I roast them in anything shallow they popped into the fire, but they could not jump out of the diploma-case."

"Well, something else seems to have jumped out of it," said the old gentleman, "and something

with which I am not satisfied. I have been looking
over these books, sir, and have read the articles on
ice, glaciers and caves, and I find no record of anything in the whole history of the world which in
the least resembles the cock-and-bull story I am
told about the butt-end of a glacier which tumbled
into a cave in your ground, and has been lying
there through all the geological ages, and the eras of
formation, and periods of animate existence down
to the days of Noah, and Moses, and Methuselah,
and Rameses II., and Alexander the Great, and
Martin Luther, and John Wesley to this day, for
you to dig out and sell to the Williamstown Ice
Company."

"But that's what happened, sir," said I.

"And besides, father," added Agnes, "the gold
and silver that people take out of mines may have
been in the ground as long as that ice has been."

"Bosh!" said Mr. Havelot. "The cases are not
at all similar. It is simply impossible that a piece
of a glacier should have fallen into a cave and been
preserved in that way. The temperature of caves
is always above the freezing-point, and that ice
would have melted a million years before you were
born."

" But, father," said Agnes, " the temperature of caves filled with ice must be very much lower than that of common caves."

" And apart from that," I added, " the ice is still there, sir."

" That doesn't make the slightest difference," he replied. " It's against all reason and common-sense that such a thing could have happened. Even if there ever was a glacier in this part of the country, and if the lower portion of it did stick out over an immense hole in the ground, that pro-truding end would never have broken off and tumbled in. Glaciers are too thick and massive for that."

" But the glacier is there, sir," said I, " in spite of your own reasoning."

" And then again," continued the old gentleman, " if there had been a cave and a projecting spur the ice would have gradually melted and dripped into the cave, and we would have had a lake and not an ice-mine. It is a perfect absurdity."

" But it's there, notwithstanding," said I.

" And you cannot subvert facts, you know father," added Agnes.

" Confound facts!" he cried. " I base my arguments on sober, cool-headed reason ; and there's nothing that can withstand reason. The thing's impossible, and, therefore, it has never happened. I went over to your place, sir, when I heard of the accident, for the misfortunes of my neighbours interest me, no matter what may be my opinion of them, and when I found that you had been extricated from your ridiculous predicament, I went through your house, and I was pleased to find it in as good or better condition than I had known it in the days of your respected father. I was glad to see the improvement in your circumstances ; but when I am told, sir, that your apparent prosperity rests upon such an absurdity as a glacier in a gravel-hill, I can but smile with contempt, sir."

I was getting a little tired of this. "But the glacier is there, sir," I said, "and I am taking out ice every day, and have reason to believe that I can continue to take it out for the rest of my life. With such facts as these before me, I am bound to say, sir, that I don't care in the least about reason."

"And I am here, father," said Agnes, coming

close to me, "and here I want to continue for the rest of my days."

The old gentleman looked at her. "And, I suppose," he said, "that you, too, don't in the least care about reason?"

"Not a bit," said Agnes.

"Well," said Mr. Havelot, rising, "I have done all I can to make you two listen to reason, and I can do no more. I despair of making sensible human beings of you, and so you might as well go on acting like a couple of ninny-hammers."

"Do ninny-hammers marry and settle on the property adjoining yours, sir?" I asked.

"Yes; I suppose they do," he said. "And when the aboriginal icehouse, or whatever the ridiculous thing is that they have discovered, gives out, I suppose that they can come to a reasonable man and ask him for a little money to buy bread and butter."

Two years have passed, and Agnes and the glacier are still mine; great blocks of ice now flow in almost a continuous stream from the mine to the railroad-station, and in a smaller, but quite as continuous stream an income flows in upon

Agnes and me ; and from one of the experimental excavations made by Tom Burton on the bluff comes a stream of ice-cold water running in a sparkling brook a-down my dell. On fine mornings before I am up, I am credibly informed that Aaron Boyce may generally be found, in season and out of season, endeavouring to catch the trout with which I am trying to stock that ice-cold stream. The diploma-case, which I caused to be carefully removed from the ice-barrier which had imprisoned me, now hangs in my study and holds our marriage certificate.

Near the line-fence which separates his property from mine, Mr. Havelot has sunk a wide shaft.

If the glacier spur under your land was a quarter of a mile wide," he says to me, " it was probably at least half a mile long ; and if that were the case, the upper end of it extends into my place, and I may be able to strike it." He has a good deal of money, this worthy Mr. Havelot, but he would be very glad to increase his riches, whether they are based upon sound reason or ridiculous facts. As for Agnes and myself, no facts or any reason could make us happier than our ardent love and our frigid fortune.

THE PHILOSOPHY OF RELATIVE EXISTENCES.

IN a certain summer, not long gone, my friend Bentley and I found ourselves in a little hamlet which overlooked a placid valley, through which a river gently moved, winding its way through green stretches until it turned the end of a line of low hills and was lost to view. Beyond this river, far away, but visible from the door of the cottage where we dwelt, there lay a city. Through the mists which floated over the valley we could see the outlines of steeples and tall roofs ; and buildings of a character which indicated thrift and business stretched themselves down to the opposite edge of the river. The more distant parts of the city, evidently a small one, lost themselves in the hazy summer atmosphere.

Bentley was young, fair-haired, and a poet ; I

was a philosopher, or trying to be one. We were good friends, and had come down into this peaceful region to work together. Although we had fled from the bustle and distractions of the town, the appearance in this rural region of a city, which, so far as we could observe, exerted no influence on the quiet character of the valley in which it lay, aroused our interest. No craft plied up and down the river; there were no bridges from shore to shore; there were none of those scattered and half-squalid habitations which generally are found on the out-skirts of a city; there came to us no distant sound of bells ; and not the smallest wreath of smoke rose from any of the buildings.

In answer to our inquiries our landlord told us that the city over the river had been built by one man, who was a visionary, and who had a great deal more money than common-sense. " It is not as big a town as you would think, sirs," he said, " because the general mistiness of things in this valley makes them look larger than they are. Those hills, for instance, when you get to them are not as high as they look to be from here. But the town is big enough, and a good deal too big ; for it ruined its builder and owner, who when he came to die had not money enough left to put up a decent tombstone at the head of his grave. He had a queer idea that he would like to have his town all finished before anybody lived in it, and so he kept on working and spending money year after year and year after year until the city was done and he had not a cent left. During all the time that the place was building hundreds of people came to him to buy houses or to hire them, but he would not listen to anything of the kind. No one must live in his town till it was all done. Even his workmen were obliged to go away at night to lodge. It is a town, sirs, I am told, in which nobody has slept for even a night. There are streets there, and places of business, and churches, and public halls, and everything that a town full of inhabitants could need; but it is all empty and deserted, and has been so as far back as I can remember, and I came to this region when I was a little boy."

"And there is no one to guard the place?" we asked; "no one to protect it from wandering vagrants who might choose to take possession of the buildings?"

" There are not many vagrants in this part of the country," he said ; "and if there were, they would not go over to that city. It is haunted."

" By what ? " we asked.

" Well, sirs, I can scarcely tell you ; queer beings that are not flesh and blood, and that is all I know about it. A good many people living hereabouts have visited that place once in their lives, but I know of no one who has gone there a second time."

" And travellers," I said ; " are they not excited by curiosity to explore that strange uninhabited city ? "

" Oh, yes," our host replied ; "almost all visitors to the valley go over to that queer city—generally in small parties, for it is not a place in which one wishes to walk about alone. Sometimes they see things, and sometimes they don't. But I never knew any man or woman show a fancy for living there, although it is a very good town."

This was said at supper-time, and, as it was the period of full moon, Bentley and I decided that we would visit the haunted city that evening. Our host endeavoured to dissuade us, saying that no one ever went over there at night ; but as we were not to be deterred, he told us where we would find his small boat tied to a stake on the river bank. We soon crossed the river, and landed at a broad, but low, stone pier, at the land end of which a line of tall grasses waved in the gentle night wind as if they were sentinels warning us from entering the silent city. We pushed through these, and walked up a street fairly wide, and so well paved that we noticed none of the weeds and other growths which generally denote desertion or little use. By the bright light of the moon we could see that the architecture was simple, and of a character highly gratifying to the eye. All the buildings were of stone and of good size. We were greatly excited and interested, and proposed to continue our walks until the moon should set, and to return on the following morning—"to live here, perhaps," said Bentley. " What could be so romantic and yet so real ? What could conduce better to the marriage of verse and philosophy ? " But as he said this we saw around the corner of a cross-street some forms as of people hurrying away.

"The spectres," said my companion, laying his hand on my arm.

"Vagrants, more likely," I answered, "who have taken advantage of the superstition of the region to appropriate this comfort and beauty to themselves."

"If that be so," said Bentley, "we must have a care for our lives."

We proceeded cautiously, and soon saw other forms fleeing before us and disappearing, as we supposed, around corners and into houses. And now suddenly finding ourselves upon the edge of a wide, open public square, we saw in the dim light—for a tall steeple obscured the moon—the forms of vehicles, horses, and men moving here and there. But before, in our astonishment, we could say a word one to the other, the moon moved past the steeple, and in its bright light we could see none of the signs of life and traffic which had just astonished us.

Timidly, with hearts beating fast, but with not one thought of turning back, nor any fear of vagrants,—for we were now sure that what we had seen was not flesh and blood, and therefore harmless,—we crossed the open space and entered a street down which the moon shone clearly.

Here and there we saw dim figures, which quickly disappeared ; but, approaching a low stone balcony in front of one of the houses, we were surprised to see, sitting thereon and leaning over a book which lay open upon the top of the carved parapet, the figure of a woman who did not appear to notice us.

"That is a real person," whispered Bentley, "and it does not see us."

"No," I replied ; "it is like the others. Let us go near it."

We drew near to the balcony and stood before it. At this the figure raised its head and looked at us. It was beautiful, it was young; but its substance seemed to be of an ethereal quality which we had never seen or known of. With its full, soft eyes fixed upon us it spoke :

"Why are you here ?" it asked. "I have said to myself that the next time I saw any of you I would ask you why you come to trouble us. Cannot you live content in your own realms and spheres, knowing, as you must know, how timid we are, and how you frighten us and make us unhappy? In all this city there is, I believe, not one of us except myself who does not flee and hide from you whenever you cruelly come here. Even I would do that, had not I declared to myself that I would see you and speak to you, and endeavour to prevail upon you to leave us in peace."

The clear, frank tones of the speaker gave me courage. "We are two men," I answered, "strangers in this region, and living for the time in the beautiful country on the other side of the river. Having heard of this quiet city, we have come to see it for ourselves. We had supposed it to be uninhabited, but now that we find that this is not the case, we would assure you from our hearts that we do not wish to disturb or annoy anyone who lives here. We simply came as honest travellers to view the city."

The figure now seated herself again, and as her countenance was nearer to us, we could see that it was filled with pensive thought. For a moment she looked at us without speaking. "Men!" she said. "And so I have been right. For a long time I have believed that the beings who sometimes come here, filling us with dread and awe, are men."

"And you," I exclaimed—"who are you, and who are these forms that we have seen, these strange inhabitants of this city?"

She gently smiled as she answered: "We are the ghosts of the future. We are the people who are to live in this city generations hence. But all of us do not know that, principally because we do not think about it and study about it enough to know it. And it is generally believed that the men and women who sometimes come here are ghosts who haunt the place."

"And that is why you are terrified and flee from us?" I exclaimed. "You think we are ghosts from another world?"

"Yes," she replied; "that is what is thought, and what I used to think."

"And you," I asked, "are spirits of human beings yet to be?"

"Yes," she answered; "but not for a long time. Generations of men, I know not how many, must pass away before we are men and women."

"Heavens!" exclaimed Bentley, clasping his hands and raising his eyes to the sky, "I shall be a spirit before you are a woman."

" Perhaps," she said again, with a sweet smile upon her face, "you may live to be very, very old."

But Bentley shook his head. This did not console him. For some minutes I stood in contemplation, gazing upon the stone pavement beneath my feet. " And this," I ejaculated, " is a city inhabited by the ghosts of the future, who believe men and women to be phantoms and spectres."

She bowed her head.

" But how is it," I asked, " that you discovered that you are spirits and we mortal men ? "

" There are so few of us who think of such things," she answered, " so few who study, ponder, and reflect. I am fond of study, and I love philosophy ; and from the reading of many books I have learned much. From the book which I have here I have learned most ; and from its teachings I have gradually come to the belief, which you tell me is the true one, that we are spirits and you men."

" And what book is that ? " I asked.

" It is ' The Philosophy of Relative Existences,' by Rupert Vance."

"Ye gods!" I exclaimed, springing upon the balcony, "that is my book, and I am Rupert Vance." I stepped toward the volume to seize it, but she raised her hand.

"You cannot touch it," she said. "It is the ghost of a book. And did you write it?"

"Write it? No," I said; "I am writing it. It is not yet finished."

"But here it is," she said, turning over the last pages. "As a spirit book it is finished. It is very successful; it is held in high estimation by intelligent thinkers; it is a standard work."

I stood trembling with emotion. "High estimation!" I said. "A standard work!"

"Oh, yes," she replied, with animation; "and it well deserves its great success, especially in its conclusion. I have read it twice."

"But let me see these concluding pages," I exclaimed. "Let me look upon what I am to write."

She smiled, and shook her head, and closed the book. "I would like to do that," she said, "but if you are really a man you must not know what you are going to do."

"Oh, tell me, tell me," cried Bentley from below, "do you know a book called 'Stellar Studies,' by Arthur Bentley? It is a book of poems."

The figure gazed at him. "No," it said presently; "I never heard of it."

I stood trembling. Had the youthful figure before me been flesh and blood, had the book been a real one, I would have torn it from her.

"O wise and lovely being!" I exclaimed, falling on my knees before her, "be also benign and generous. Let me but see the last page of my book. If I have been of benefit to your world; more than all, if I have been of benefit to you, let me see, I implore you—let me see how it is that I have done it."

She rose with the book in her hand. "You have only to wait until you have done it," she said, "and then you will know all that you could see here." I started to my feet, and stood alone upon the balcony.

"I AM sorry," said Bentley, as we walked toward the pier where we had left our boat, "that we talked only to that ghost girl, and that the other spirits were all afraid of us. Persons whose souls are choked up with philosophy are not apt to care much for poetry ; and even if my book is to be widely known, it is easy to see that she may not have heard of it."

I walked triumphant. The moon, almost touching the horizon, beamed like red gold. " My dear friend," said I, " I have always told you that you should put more philosophy into your poetry. That would make it live."

" And I have always told you," said he, "that you should not put so much poetry into your philosophy. It misleads people."

" It didn't mislead that ghost girl," said I.

" How do you know ? " said he. " Perhaps she is wrong, and the other inhabitants of the city are right, and we may be the ghosts after all. Such things, you know, are only relative. Anyway," he continued, after a little pause, " I wish I knew that those ghosts were now reading the poem I am going to begin to-morrow."

THE KNIFE THAT KILLED PO HANCY.

PO HANCY was the chief of a band of Dacoit robbers, those outlaws who for years
have ravished portions of British Burmah, killing,
stealing, and burning, and regarding not whether
the sufferers were their own people or white-
skinned foreigners. Prominent among these midnight assassins and robbers was Po Hancy. But he
came to his just reward at last, being trapped and
killed by two native spies, and the knife by which
his head was severed from his body lay on my library
table. It had been sent to me by a missionary
friend to whom it had been brought as a trophy of
the superior valour of the loyal and somewhat
civilised natives over that of the outlaws of the
jungle. It was a rude weapon, with a heavy blade
nearly nine inches long, enclosed in a wooden

sheath, and with a beautifully polished handle of bone-like wood. On the point of the blade and on its sides were great blotches of rust, caused by the blood of Po Hancy.

This formidable weapon, with its history, was very interesting to me. I could sympathise with the joyful satisfaction with which the little band of missionaries had looked upon the knife as a blessed sleep-giver, an assurance that they no longer lie awake on account of rumours of the approach of that bloodthirsty and inconvertible heathen and his band.

More than that, it had another interest for me. It made me think of the man who had come to his death by it. The idea struck me that Po Hancy and I were as different from each other as two human beings could possibly be. To arrange our differences in a tabulated statement would be a work of a good deal of time and very little value, but there was one dissimilarity between us that particularly impressed itself upon me. I had heard a good deal of this tiger-like Dacoit, crawling through the jungles for ten, fifteen, or twenty miles, leaping down rocks with foothold as silent and certain as that of a cat, and bounding upon his victims with a strength and swiftness of an untiring beast of prey.

How different was I—a languid, soft-fleshed, almost middle-aged lawyer, tired out by sedentary work by night and by day, to whom a walk of half-a-mile was weariness, and a climb to my office on the fifth floor of a lofty building was a backache. As a young man I had been somewhat athletic, but years of too much work of one kind, and too little of another, had made activity a memory, and wholesome exercise a discomfort. Po Hancy was a specimen of perfect animal life, and of the most imperfect life of the mind and soul. My body resembled his mind and soul; of my mind and soul I will say nothing, being of a modest disposition.

Po Hancy was gone, utterly departed and annihilated with the exception of the atoms of dried blood which might yet remain in the blotches of rust upon this ugly knife-blade. Strangely enough, it was possible that something which helped to make up that fierce Dacoit, some portions, minute though they might be, of his very self, might lie here before me in my library, by my prayer book, and a recent letter from my mother in a home of high civilisation on the other side the world from the Burmese jungle.

As I sat thinking of these things I took out my pocket-knife, and began to scratch the spots of rust upon the blade, and succeeding in detaching a little of the fine dust from the iron, oxidised by means of Po Hancy's life currents. There was so little of it, that I had to moisten the end of my knife-blade in order to take it up, and carefully look at it. Of course to the eye it was like any other iron rust, but to my mind it was far different. If there really were still atoms of blood on it, it was all, or nearly all, that remained above earth of the famous Po Hancy.

Involuntarily I balanced my penknife on my finger, as if to weigh this infinitesimal remnant of savage mortality, when suddenly the knife slipped, and, in endeavouring to catch it, the point ran into the thumb of my left hand, inflicting a slight wound. For a moment I was frightened. Here was an example of the folly of playing with edged tools, especially those that had belonged to savage heathens. This knife of the slayer of the Dacoit might have been poisoned, and here I had wounded myself with the point of my own knife, to which adhered the dust I had scraped from it. It was horrible to think that in a few hours I might perish by the same knife that slew that ferocious murderer.

After a time, however, I calmed myself, for I had never heard that the Burmese used poisoned weapons, and when several days had passed without my having felt any evil effects from the wound, which soon healed, I felt perfectly safe. In fact, instead of there being any injurious result from the cut (or the not inconsiderable nervous shock consequent upon it), I found myself in better health than usual, and one afternoon I walked across the Common, through the Public Garden, and four or five blocks beyond, to my home, and did not feel the least fatigue. I had had no experience of this kind for two or three years.

During the next few weeks, many of my friends remarked that my health was certainly improving, and there could be no doubt that they were correct. I began to take walks that were moderately long. I played billiards, that used to tire me so much that I seldom played a whole game. And what surprised everybody, and myself quite as much, I joined an athletic club. This numbered among its members a dozen or more of my friends, nearly all of whom, at one time or another, had pressed me to join the club, assuring me that it was the best thing I could do, if I wished to regain my old strength and activity, but I had always refused. The very idea of gymnastic exercise was disagreeable to me, and I was annoyed at their persistence in advising it.

Now they were astonished at my change of opinion, and some of them were inclined to ridicule me, suggesting some very easy and mild methods of exercise suitable for a small boy beginner. But they stopped that sort of chaff when I raised a vaulting bar several inches higher than the last performer had left it, and then went over it without touching, and when, seizing a trapeze bar, I drew up my body, and threw myself around it with the ease of a circus man, some of them remembered that I used to do that sort of thing, but that I could return to it now, after all these years of desk work, amazed them.

I kept up my gymnastic exercises nearly every day, and as the club was to give a public exhibition early in the autumn, I felt inclined to take part in it. All my love for athletic sport had returned. But, in spite of my undoubted activity, there were a good many men in the club who were greatly my superiors in athletic feats, and there was no reason to suppose that I would achieve any especial distinction in the public games. The conviction of this somewhat dampened my desire to become a contestant on so important an occasion, and I sat down one evening to consider the matter. "In the first place," I said to myself, "how did I regain all my old strength and activity? I have not altered my method of living, my diet is the same, I have had no change of air." At this moment my eye fell on the knife that killed Po Hancy, which still lay upon my table. "By George!" I exclaimed, springing to my feet, "could it have been that?"

My face flushed and my whole form glowed as I remembered how I had fancied I had poisoned myself by introducing into my veins the stuff I had scraped from the Burmese knife. And now,

could it be? Was it by any means possible that I
had accidentally inoculated myself with some of
the blood of Po Hancy, and in so doing had intro-
duced into my system some of his savage vigour
and agility !

The more I thought of this the more strongly I
became convinced that it was so. I am a scientist
in an amateur way, and I take a great interest in
experiments such as those performed by Brown-
Sequard and Dr. Koch. If certain physical at-
tributes of one class of living beings could be
communicated to another by inoculation or hyper-
dermic injection, why should not another physical
attribute be transmitted in the same way? I could
see no reason why this should not be so, and, in
fact, I believed myself a proof that the thing could
be done.

Now, if I possessed some of the high physical
qualities of the defunct Po Hancy, why should I
not possess them to a greater degree ? What he
had in perfection was what I lacked. If I could
get what he no longer needed, and what, indeed, I
would gladly have deprived him of, whether I had
been able to get it or not, why should I not have it?

There was really nothing to object to in this proposition, and I determined to make an experiment.

Rubbing some glycerine over the blood spots upon the Dacoit knife, I scraped vigorously until I accumulated a little mass of the gummy substance. Then baring my left arm, and excoriating a little spot on it, as if I were about to vaccinate myself, I rubbed in the compound. " Now," said I, wrapping a handkerchief around my arm, "we shall see what we shall see."

The next morning, our waitress, who was just entering the breakfast-room, saw what she did see. She saw me come in at another door, look at the table set ready for the family breakfast with a large bouquet, a foot and a half high, in the centre of the table, run a few steps, and then bound entirely over said table, bouquet and all, and come down upon the other side with an elastic thud as if I had been made of india-rubber. She screamed, and although I had not touched anything, stood expecting a crash.

" Merciful me, sir," she exclaimed, when she found nothing was about to happen, " I never did see anybody so supple."

When my two sisters came down—with me they made up the family, for my mother was in Europe —I had to tell them about this jump, for I did not want the girl to do it.

" I have noticed, Harry," said Amelia, "that you have changed very much of late. You are as springy as a jack-in-a-box, and you used to be so pokey and stiff. I think you ought not to do that sort of thing in the house. Suppose you had swept everything off this table, what a lot of damage you would have done. And I have had to have the stair-carpet stretched and replaced because you will persist in going up three steps at a time, and getting it all out of shape."

" I am very glad that Harry is feeling so strong and well," said Jenny, "and I am going to teach him to play tennis."

I laughed internally as I thought of a man with my nimble power playing a baby game like tennis.

The inoculation with the blood of Po Hancy was undoubtedly a success. I could feel strength and vigour bounding through my veins ; without hesitation I announced myself as a candidate for athletic honours in the approaching games.

I will not here relate the feats I performed on the great field of our club. In contests of hurling, lifting, and all that I took no part, but in running, jumping, vaulting, bounding, I excelled all competitors and broke several records. Had Po Hancy been in my place he might have done better, but without the influence of Po Hancy's wild blood no one on the grounds could have done as well. This is what I said to myself as the crowd roared out its applause, and my friends gathered around me to shake my hand.

Not only was my whole habit of life changed, but the changes went on. I was not content to be able to bound like a tiger, and run like a deer, but I wanted to do these things. Several times when coming home from my office in the evening I was stopped by policemen, who wanted to know what I was running away from. I had some difficulty in persuading them that I ran purely from a love of exercise, and they advised against such speed in the public streets. Late at night I used to have grand runs on the Common, but this did not suit me very well. There were sometimes observers, and the place was too open. I liked better the public gardens, which afterwards became my nightly exercise ground.

With a pair of soft tennis-shoes on my feet, it was my delight to steal swiftly around masses of shrubbery, dart up avenues, slip before the eyes of astonished policemen, and vanish into the shade, to bound into the branches of some heavily-foliaged tree and watch the guardian of the peace stalking below me, and then when he had passed to drop noiselessly down, to track him over the whole of his beat, without his suspecting that my soft falling footsteps followed his.

I did not pay much attention to my business, as had been my custom, and I indulged in exercise and long walks even in the day-time, when I should have been at my office. I felt a great desire to hunt ; I do not mean to follow the hounds in their courses about the Boston suburbs, but to tramp through the wild woods and kill things with a rifle. As there was little scope for this sort of sport in the coast country of Massachusetts, I wanted to take a trip to the lower part of Florida, for it was too late in the season to go far west. In the forest down there I was sure I could still find wild game, and if a wandering Seminole Indian happened to interfere with me, or a reckless alligator hunter picked a quarrel with me, I felt that I would be very well able to take care of myself.

My law partners, however, objected very strongly to my leaving town in the midst of our busiest season, and I was obliged to postpone my contemplated trip. One of the members of our firm jocosely remarked to me that so far as business was concerned I was a better man when I was not so well. And my sisters, who used to object to walking with me because I was so much given to going slowly and stopping often, now declined to accompany me because I strode so rapidly that it tired them to keep up with me. In fact, in the whole of Boston I did not know anyone who shared my fancies for what might be called super-exercise, and I was obliged to be content with my own company in my morning bounces and my evening spins.

But it must not be supposed that I lost at this time my desire for companionship; in truth a novel desire of that sort sprung up within me. A distant relative of my mother, who had always been accustomed to spend some weeks with us in the autumn, now came to make her annual visit. This was a lady of thirty or thereabouts, by the name of Susan Mooney. She was the kindest, gentlest, quietest, softest woman in the world. Her disposition was so tender that if one spoke to her of trouble or pain the tears would almost always come into her eyes.

My sisters were sorry that Susan had made her visit this year during the absence of our mother, for although they liked her and loved her, they did not find her a congenial companion. They were lively girls, fond of society, while she was the quietest of the quiet, and fond of home. Consequently they were well pleased when they found that I seemed to fancy Susan's company, for that relieved them of the burden. But after a week or two, their feelings changed, and they told me they thought I was giving entirely too much of my time to Susan. My family had come to look upon me as a bachelor who would never think of marrying, and it would have surprised them to see me paying marked attention to any lady. But when my sisters saw me paying attention so very marked indeed to Susan Mooney, they were not only surprised but offended.

"If you are going to marry anybody," said Amelia, "do take someone who is suitable for you. Mother is very fond of Susan, and we like her, but she would never do for a wife for you. She is nothing but a bag of milk."

I looked at them and smiled. It was true that I had taken Susan to the theatre or concerts, evening after evening, although I had been in the habit of declining to go to such places with my sisters ; that I made her take long walks with me : that I spent hours with her when I should have been in my office, and that lately she had been seen to flush a little when I came into the room where she was.

"Susan Mooney," said I, "is exactly the kind of girl—or lady—that I like. She is so gentle, so docile, so submissive, that——"

"Submissive!" snapped Jenny, "I should think so. She has not the least bit of will of her own. You would become a perfect tyrant with a wife like that. I believe she would grow to tremble when she heard your footstep."

"I do not say," I answered, "that I am going to marry Susan, nor that I am going to marry anybody, but if I ever do take a wife, I want one who will tremble when she hears my footstep."

They both laughed. "For a mild-mannered man," cried Amelia, "you talk bigger than anyone I ever heard. The idea that anyone could ever tremble at your footstep is ridiculous."

I made no answer. It was well that they could not analyze the blood that now ran in my veins. To me Susan Mooney was attractive to a degree that no other woman had been. I would not cease my attentions to her, but, perhaps, since my sisters seemed so observant, I would be more wary about them.

I had used to be somewhat of a submissive person myself, but I was such no longer. I did not always state my determination to do things against the opinions and wishes of others, but the determination was never altered. I grew to like to put myself in opposition, especially if the other party did not know how I stood. This, I flattered myself, might be a good thing for a lawyer, but it was very different from my old methods of thought

and action. I also felt occasional desires to put
myself in physical opposition to someone. I did
not feel quarrelsome, but if I had seen a reasonable opportunity of obtruding my physical superiority on a fellow being, I should have been glad to
avail myself of it. Civilised society does not offer
chances of this sort sufficiently often to satisfy Po
Hanic cravings.

One evening as I was sitting in my library and
study on the third floor, I heard a slight noise
downstairs, as if from the opening of a door. I
knew that the rest of the family had all retired, and
I naturally thought that a burglar was trying to
enter the house. The moment this idea came
into my mind, my whole body thrilled with a warm
ecstasy. I slipped off my shoes, and stole to the
top of the stairs and listened—I heard the noise
again! Darting back into my room, I buttoned
my dark coat tight round my neck to conceal my
white collar, and then, seizing the knife that killed
Po Hancy, I silently glided down the stairway.
My eyes must have glistened with the expectant
joy of meeting a burglar. What transporting
delight it would be to steal upon the rascal and

slay him with one blow. It is so seldom that one
gets an opportunity to legitimately slay a rascal
or, indeed, anyone. I do not say that I could
have decoyed a burglar into the house for the purpose of slaying him, but if one were really here of
his own accord, how gladly would I exercise my
legal rights.

Down the stairs I went, bending low, with eyes
peering into the dark, with ears stretched to catch
the slightest sound, and with the knife that killed
Po Hancy half raised in my right hand. I went
through all the rooms on the first floor, I descended
into the cellar, feeling my way about in the darkness, and stopping at intervals to listen. I even
penetrated to the back of the coal bin, and I
remember thinking with pride how I stepped so
carefully as to scarcely disturb the coals that were
piled about me.

Suddenly I heard the same noise that I had
noticed before. It was above me, and with a
quick and silent bound I was at the top of the
cellar stairs. Here I found what had made the
noise; it was a door at this spot which had been
left open. I noticed that it was not fastened when

I came down, but thought nothing of it. A ventilating window was near by, and when a puff of wind came into this window the door was opened a little way and then slowly swung back of its own inclination.

When I discovered the facts of the case I could almost have cried. I felt that I had sustained a cruel disappointment. Chagrined and depressed, I walked slowly into the dining-room and sat down, debating with myself whether or not I would care to put on my hat and take a long night run. While sitting thus I heard someone coming down the stairs with slow and deliberate footsteps. I knew those footsteps; they were those of Mary Carpenter, our good old housekeeper. Ashamed that she should find me sitting in the dark, I got up and began to look for matches, but before I found them she entered, carrying a lighted candle.

" Mercy on me, Mr. Harry!" she exclaimed, " what on earth are you doing here in the dark? I just remembered that I did not fasten the top cellar door, and I came down to do it. Are you sick?"

" No," I answered; " I am hungry, and I came

down to get some pie. I was just going to strike a light."

"Well, well!" exclaimed the good Mary, "that is just like you, Mr. Harry. When you were a boy, and even a young man, you were always wanting to eat pie at night, and there were some that said that you would have had better health if you had not done so much of it. But for my part, I can't see any harm in eating good wholesome pie, when a body feels hungry for it. I have not heard you say you wanted some pie for a long while, and it seems like good old times to give you some after everybody else is in bed. Now, it is lucky that I made to-day with my own hands the first pumpkin pies of the season. I'll get one and cut you a piece. Goodness gracious, Mr. Harry! you didn't mean to cut one of my pies with that horrible knife, did you? If you did I am truly glad that I came down in time to stop you. A heathen knife in a Christian pie is something I never heard of yet, and I hope never to. It would poison it."

In a few minutes the good Mary placed before me a noble specimen of her pastry cooking.

"There," said she, "is a pumpkin pie fit for a king, only kings never get them; and I suppose they would call it a pudding in England, if they had it at all. It's a good inch and a half thick, the way you always liked them, and I am sure a piece of it will not hurt you."

She cut a generous segment of the pie and gave it to me on a plate. She was delighted to see with what pleasure I ate it, and when I asked for another piece she was surprised, but gave it to me.

When I asked for a third piece she demurred a little, but in spite of her really earnest protestations I helped myself to more, and eventually finished the whole pie, which was of a size sufficient for an ordinary family.

"Well, well," said Mary, as she took away my plate and the empty pie-dish, "this beats anything you ever did when you were a boy. I only hope that you won't feel badly in the night; but if you do, come to my door and knock. It won't take me a minute to mix some peppermint for you, or give you anything else you need."

I did not wonder that the good Mary was astonished at the midnight appetite of a Po

Hancy. I began to fear, however, that I had been imprudent in letting this appetite run away with me, and felt very glad that there was some-one in the house who knew what to do for victims of unreasonable voracity. However, there was no occasion for her services, for I went to bed and slept the sleep of an infant. In the morning when I awoke, fresh and clear-headed, with a wholesome appetite for my breakfast, I felt what it was to possess the digestion of a Dacoit.

The wonderful physical powers with which I felt myself endowed were sources of the greatest satisfaction to me; but they began to have their drawbacks, and after a time they caused me great mental uneasiness. Because I knew myself per-fectly able to do certain things which I ought not to do, I wished to do them. For instance, there was a stout man of German Jewish aspect, who, before my Po Hanic days, had been in the habit of going home from his business about the same time that I did, and frequently took the street car in which I was riding. This man, if it were possible, always seated himself next to me, think-ing, I imagined, that as I was rather a slender man, he would have a better chance of crowding me, and getting more than his share of room in case the car became full. And when this opportunity was afforded him he always availed himself of it to the utmost. I sometimes remonstrated with him, and sometimes tried to crowd him a little, but neither course was of any service, and it not unfrequently happened that I got up and stood on the platform to avoid this unsavoury persecutor.

As I now thought of this man, my blood boiled within me. I did not, at this time, ride in street cars, for I felt no need of them, but I felt greatly tempted to get into one at the hour I usually left my office, in the hope that the stout man would enter and sit beside me. If this should happen and he should dare to push or elbow me, I would spring upon him and hurl him out of the door of the car, no matter how rapidly it might be moving. I ground my teeth in savage anticipation of the joy I would take in thus avenging myself for all his former insults. But my common sense and my familiarity with the common law showed me that this would be a very foolish thing to do, certain to bring me into trouble, and even ridicule, which would be worse. My uncivilised instincts were so strong that frequently I was obliged, figuratively, to put my hand upon my own shoulder to prevent myself from entering a car in which there was a chance of encountering the stout German.

There were other novel and perhaps aboriginal cravings which came upon me at this time. One of these was an abnormal longing to possess desirable objects. For instance, in a jeweller's window which I frequently passed, there was a handsome brooch which attracted my favourable attention. It was composed of a large stone of the moonstone order, artissically surrounded by brilliants. It struck me that this would be a most appropriate ornament for the gentle Susan, and several times I stood looking at it and planning how I might get it for her, without resort to the usual methods of exchange. A strong tap on the window pane, a quick snatch, and then a series of dartings and doublings, along a route which I had marked out in my mind,—around a corner, up an alley, over the fences of two back yards that I had noted, into a small street, where I would change my soft, light coloured felt hat for a dark travelling cap which I would have in my pocket. Then a rush into a crowded thoroughfare, and a leisurely walk home. But this scheme did not altogether please me ; I would have better liked, in the dark hours of the morning, to climb a tree which stood before the jeweller's shop, to go out on a limb until it bent down to the level of the transom window over the top of the door, to open this, slip in, pocket the brooch, climb up to the transom, listen, drop outside, and noiselessly glide away.

I had entirely too many fancies of this kind, and when away from my temptations, my mind was seriously troubled by the thoughts of the dangers to which I was exposed ; this robber blood was making a different man of me, a man who ran the risk of ending his life in a prison. I used to ponder for hours upon my alarming condition. Sometimes I thought of myself as another Mr. Hyde, but alas ! my case was worse than that. I was not sometimes good, and sometimes bad ; I was under an influence which was steadfast and of increasing power, the effects of which, my reason told me, must be permanent. When a Christian gentleman puts Dacoit blood into his veins there is no way of his getting it out again, except by letting out all of his blood, a remedy I did not fancy. How earnestly I wished Po Hancy had been converted before he had been killed.

But had the robber chief repented and lived a proper life, he would not have been killed, and I would have had no knife with his blood on it, and my present physical perfection would never have come to me. When I looked upon the matter in this light I asked myself whether I would have been satisfied had it been so, and I could not bring myself to answer " yes." After all it was my vanity that had brought this terrible peril upon me. Had I been contented with the little prick my knife had given me I might have been no more than the active, healthy gentleman I had always wished to be. But that foolish desire to shine in the athletic games had not only given me an excess of strength, but also the impulses of a jungle sneak.

When troubled thus, my greatest relief was the society of Susan Mooney. The flow of her gentle soul was so unrippled that it seldom failed to soothe me. Feeling the great good she was to me

I now made up my mind to marry her, and it delighted me to think that in doing so I would not be troubled by the ordinary antecedents of matrimony. I would simply inform her that she was to be my wife, then all she would have to do was to set herself to the task of getting ready for the ceremony. But I could not always avail myself of the soothings of Susan, and the agitation of my mind became more harassing and frequent.

Early one evening I was sitting alone in my study, torn by a desire to take a long walk in the suburbs, and restrained by a fear that if I did so I should be induced to forget that I was not a prowling Dacoit. Suddenly I heard a cry below stairs ; it was the voice of my dear Susan, in terror and pain. In ten seconds I had bounded down to the drawing-room, where, between my two sisters I found the fair Susan almost fainting, with one of her white hands reddened with her blood, and in her lap the knife that killed Po Hancy. The situation quickly explained ; that afternoon Jenny had brought down the knife to show a visitor interested in such things, and now Susan had been playing with it and had cut her finger !

The wound was not a serious one, and the sufferer was soon cared for and conducted to her room. I took the knife upstairs, determined to lock it up securely. But as I was about to replace it in its sheath I noticed that the blade was discoloured in several places with fresh blood—the blood of Susan still moist.

I sat for some ten minutes earnestly gazing upon the knife-blade. What a contrast—the blood of Po Hancy, the blood of Susan Mooney. As I pondered, a thought, seemingly filled with the light of salvation, dawned upon me. I bared my right arm, and with my penknife scratched the skin for the space of over an inch in diameter. On this I rubbed the moist blood of Susan, as much of it as I could get from the great knife-blade, and which exceeded in quantity that which I had obtained from the rust spots. I trembled when this deed was finished, I did not dare to think what might happen, but I hoped.

The next day my right arm was very sore and I could not write. I felt sure that no one with Dacoit blood in his veins should be allowed to perform an operation of the nature of vaccination.

As my disability, the cause of which I did not explain to anyone, gave a reason for a little vacation, I went off to the Berkshire hills. The gay season of Stockbridge and Lennox had not yet come to an end, and the life there interested me very much. It was a pleasant change; for years I had mingled very little in fashionable society. I met a good many friends and acquaintances, all glad to have me with them, but surprised as well as pleased at my willingness to enter into all the festive doings of the region. In fact, I agreed to whatever was proposed to me, except when two of my fellow members of the athletic club asked me to join them in a long tramp. This I declined, mainly for the reason that they had planned to start very early in the morning, before sunrise, and I would not give up the delightful and tranquillising hours of sleep which immediately precede a late breakfast.

At the close of the day after my return I rode home from my office in a street car. At the corner where I had been in the habit of expecting him, the stout German got in. There was an empty place next to me, large enough for an ordinary person, but not large enough for him. He came directly toward me and endeavoured to squeeze himself into the vacancy. As he did so I moved as far as possible away from him, in order to give him the room he desired.

That evening my sister Amelia took me aside. " Harry," said she, "I have something very serious to say to you. Susan has had a letter from mother begging her to stay here until her return. Now, this will keep her with us a month longer at least, and I think this is a very deplorable thing."

" Why so?" I asked.

" Because it will give you an opportunity to carry on your absurd courtship of her, and that cannot fail to end in your marrying her, and I should like to know, Harry, what could be more deplorable than that ? In fact, Jenny and I have made up our minds that we will not stand it. Mother may consent to live in the house with that simple Susan as your wife, but we never will.

" My dear sister," said I, " you and Jenny need not trouble yourselves on that subject. I do not in the least desire to marry Susan Mooney. She is a good woman, very good, but she is not the sort of person I would want for a wife. I should think you could see that for yourselves. The life of a hard-working man like myself is monotonous enough without Susan. But now that you have spoken of marriage I will say that I met two ladies, one in Stockbridge and the other at Lennox, either of which would make me a good wife. I rather prefer the Lennox girl, Miss Camilla Sunderland. Do you know her?"

"Camilla Sunderland!" exclaimed my sister. "She is a leading belle, a dazzling star of the season. She goes everywhere, does everything, driving four-in-hand, plays tennis matches, is devoted to balls, theatre parties—why, my dear Harry, I should think you could not exist with a wife like that."

"Miss Sunderland," said I, leaning back in a soft armchair, "would be just the wife I dream of. I am sure I prefer her to the lady at Stockbridge. I am not disposed, as you know, to take part to any great extent in the exciting life of the fashionable world, but I should wish to feel that through my wife I had a part in it."

"Well!" exclaimed Amelia, "you may never

get Camilla Sunderland, but I am truly glad that you have given up all thoughts of Susan. But, Harry, a very great change must have come over you ; it was not long ago that you told me you wanted a wife who would tremble at your tread."

I made a gesture of languid disapprobation. " Dear girl," said I, "I should despise a woman who would tremble at my tread."

I have not yet married Miss Sunderland, partly because it is difficult for a man of my quiet and slow turn of mind to follow and find her in the mazes and intricacies of the fashionable life in which she exists, and partly because my sisters have succeeded in making me doubt her acceptance of my addresses in case I should get the opportunity of offering them to her. But I want her, and until she is married to somebody else, I shall continue to hope.

As for the knife that killed Po Hancy, I threw it into the Charles River. It was a dangerous knife.

THE REV. EZEKIEL CRUMP.

IT was one o'clock on a bright October day, and Mr. Nathan Rinkle had just sat down to dinner, with Mrs. Nicely Lent on the other side of the table. The day was warm for the season, and Mr. Rinkle, having been very busy since early morning, had a good appetite. But he had barely made one deep cut into the leg of mutton before him when the door opened, and a boy with an old straw hat on his head came in. He hesitated for a moment as if he thought he should make some apology for breaking in upon the sanctity of the dinner hour, and then he said :

" I've just come to tell you that I think the Rev'rend Ezekiel Crump is dyin'. He's all doubled up."

" Gracious ! " exclaimed Mr. Rinkle, suddenly pushing back his chair, " I must go out this

minute. It's the heat. I didn't count on its being
so extra warm to-day." And with this he clapped
on his hat and left the house.

"Oh, dear!" exclaimed Mrs. Lent, as she gazed
at the table she had arranged with so much care,
" I suppose I might as well put these things by the
fire to keep 'em warm. There's no knowin' when
he'll be back. I wish that boy Joe had kept away
until dinner was over. But I suppose it couldn't
be helped. It would never do to let the Rev.
Ezekiel die."

Nathan Rinkle was a florist, and the Rev.
Ezekiel Crump was a new and fine pelargonium
which had been originated by Mr. Rinkle himself,
and which he had named for the reverend gentleman who had married his father and mother, and
baptised him. Mr. Rinkle had often said that this
good man's name would be given to the finest new
flower he should ever grow; and as he did not
believe he should produce anything better than
this pelargonium, the name was given to it.

Nathan was a tall, slim, muscular bachelor of
about forty, industrious and devoted to his profession, and a respected member of society in the

country region in which he lived. Mrs. Lent, a well-nurtured lady, whose age hovered around thirty-five, was the widow of Mr. Rinkle's former partner. The house belonged to Mr. Rinkle, and he, with Joshua Lent and his wife, lived in it very pleasantly and profitably for five or six years. When Joshua died three years ago this autumn, Nathan was not the man to turn his widow out of doors ; so Mrs. Lent, who now owned a certain share in the business, remained as housekeeper and general domestic manager. And, thus far, the arrangement had been found pleasant and profitable to all parties concerned.

It was half an hour before Mr. Rinkle returned from the greenhouse, and as Mrs. Lent had seen him coming, the dinner was again on the table when he entered.

"It wasn't as bad as Joe thought it was," he said, as he took his seat at the table, "but it was bad enough. I think I have been too careful with that plant, a little too careful. I've been sparing with the water on it. I didn't want it to bloom too fast. I wanted the three sprays I left on it to be absolutely perfect for the flower show to-morrow and I was so busy this morning getting the other things ready I didn't look at the Rev. Ezekiel, and as he was in a pretty hot place for such a day, and too dry about the roots, he began to wilt. But I think he is all right now. I've given him a good soaking, and put him in the shade, and he began to brighten up before I left him. I tell you, Mrs. Lent, that gave me a real shock."

"As well it might," said the sympathetic Nicely.

That afternoon Mrs. Lent went out to the greenhouses to look at the wonderful new pelargonium. She found the reverend gentleman fully restored to health, strength, and beauty, and she felt quite convinced that never had the eye of man rested upon so grand and glorious a pelargonium. And, furthermore, there could be no imaginable reason to doubt that on the morrow Mr. Rinkle would receive a first prize.

When Mr. Rinkle with his lantern came in from the greenhouses that evening, he told Mrs. Lent that he should go out several times during the night to see if everything was all right; and that he should leave very early the next morning for the town, about ten miles away, where the flower show was to be held.

"I'm going to send Joe off with one waggon at daylight, and then, as soon as I can get off, I shall follow with the other, which won't be more than half full; so I am going to stop at the Widow Sharp's and take along the plants she's got to show, for she hasn't any way of getting them there herself."

"Do you mean," asked Nicely, anxiously, "that you are going before breakfast?"

"Oh yes," said Nathan, "and as I've got to stop at the Widow Sharp's any way I'll breakfast there."

"And I suppose, of course, that you'll take the Rev. Ezekiel with you?"

"Oh, yes, indeed," answered Nathan, "you may be sure I will take charge of that plant. That pelargonium is going to make a commotion at the show, I can tell you. I've got a lot of young plants of it, but I didn't expect I'd have one bloom this year. This one is a little spindling, it is true, but he's got three sprays of flowers which are finer than anybody has ever yet seen on a pelargonium plant."

" I'm so glad you are able to exhibit it so much sooner than you expected," said Mrs. Lent. " That ought to be a good thing for you."

" I've no doubt it will be," said Nathan, taking up his candle. " I'll leave Gottlieb Stein in charge of the greenhouses to-morrow, and I'll tell him to come up to the house now and then to see if you want anything. He'll come at seven o'clock and I'll see him before I go. Good night."

In the early dawn of the next morning the boy Joe started for the show with the grey mare and a well-loaded wagon ; and at seven o'clock Nathan Rinkle began to be impatient for the coming of his chief assistant, Gottlieb Stein, who lived about a mile away. He wanted him to put the brown horse to the covered waggon, in a back corner of which the Rev. Ezekiel was to travel, carefully protected from the cool morning air ; and he had many directions to give his assistant for the conduct of his establishment during the day.` It was seldom that Gottlieb was late in coming to his work, and Nathan was much annoyed that he should happen to be so on this important occasion.

After fuming and fretting for at least a quarter

of an hour as he walked up and down the principal greenhouse, gathering together the plants he
meant to take to the show, the thought struck him
that possibly Gottlieb might have forgotten what
was to be the great business of the day and had
gone to work in some of the other houses. So he
hastily ran out to look for him. He opened the
doors of two other greenhouses, looked in and
called, but the man was not in either of them ;
then he ran over to the violet-house, which was
newer than the other houses and at some distance
from them. Mr. Rinkle did not find there the man
he wanted to see, but he found something he did
not want to see, and that was that a number of the
violet beds were very much in need of water.

"Confound it !" he ejaculated, "here is a piece
of forgetfulness. And while I'm waiting for that
fellow I might as well freshen up these beds," and
taking up a watering-pot, he proceeded to the
cistern.

This reservoir, supplied with rain water from the
roof, was simply a wide hole, about nine feet deep,
in the central part of the house. It had been dug
in a bed of clay, and the inside of it had not yet

been walled up or cemented, for as Mr. Rinkle had found its clay sides and bottom impervious to water, and it made a very good cistern as it was, he had postponed finishing it for the present. As the cistern was yet uncovered, no pump had been placed in it, and Gottlieb had found it easy enough to draw water from it by means of a bucket and rope. So now, as he had to take Gottlieb's place, Nathan Rinkle crouched down to the edge of the cistern and lowered the bucket. Gottlieb Stein was a heavy-footed man, and had crouched at that spot so often that the earth was a little depressed and inclined cistern-ward, and Mr. Rinkle's over-shoes being wet with the morning dew, were slippery. In consequence, before the bucket was half-way down, Mr. Rinkle slipped into the cistern himself, and arrived with a great splash at the bottom.

Plunged thus suddenly into darkness and water, the good gardener's surprise almost took away his breath. Fortunately he came down in a stand-ing position, and as soon as he was able to command his senses he discovered that, although a good deal jarred, he had not been hurt. He also discovered, to his great surprise, that the water was very low, and that it did not come up to the top of the rubber overshoes which he wore to protect the well-blacked boots he had put on for the flower show. The season had been dry, and but little rain had run into the cistern, and it might be that the difficulty of dipping with a bucket in two or three inches of water would explain Gottlieb's remissness in the matter of watering the violets.

Nathan's first impulse was to wade around the sides of the cistern and endeavour to find some means of climbing out. This was instinctively natural but impossible. The walls, although not quite perpendicular, were smooth and slippery.

Then, at the top of his voice, Nathan began to call for help, but after indulging in this exercise for some time he was forced to admit to himself that it was useless. The door of the violet-house was shut, and as it was at a considerable distance from any other building, it was not at all likely that he could make anybody hear him until Gottlieb, not finding his employer anywhere else, should come to that building to look for him.

Nathan's anger more than filled the cistern. He

was not a swearing man, but if the dilatory Gottlieb could have heard the threats of his employer and could have seen the clenched fist he shook in the air, he would probably have been afraid to go to his assistance. But as he could do nothing but wait, Nathan thought he might as well wait as comfortably as possible, so he laid hold of the bucket, and, turning it bottom upwards, sat down upon it. He drew his coat tails over his knees, and as his feet were protected by his overshoes, he was enabled thus to sit without getting wet.

It was not cold in the cistern, for the air was tempered by the greenhouse temperature above, and although it was very damp, Mr. Rinkle did not mind that. He had passed so many years of his life in moist glasshouses, going from their heat out into the cold and dampness of the outer air without any change of clothing, that his skin had become tough and hardened, and he never thought of such a thing as taking cold. As he sat thus and considered his misfortunes, he was still very angry, but he did not despair. Even if Gottlieb did not make his appearance until eight o'clock, it would still be time enough for him to start with his flowers for

the show; and so he sat and sat until, as his sleep
had been very broken the night before, he fell into
a doze. With his hands folded in his lap, and his
chin on his breast, he slept as he had often done
during the night watches in his greenhouses.

While Mr. Rinkle slept Mrs. Nicely Lent was at
work in her kitchen. She was a pleasant-looking
woman, of a cheerful temperament, and yet as she
worked she heaved a little sigh. Her breakfast
was over and she was preparing the mincemeat for
the first mince pie of the season, and was doing it
with great care, for Mr. Rinkle was fond of mince
pies, and would gladly welcome this unexpected
harbinger of the season of good eating.

Moreover, it was Mrs. Lent's birthday, and she
saw no better way of celebrating it than by making
something good for Mr. Rinkle. It was quite
certain that no one would think of making anything
good for her. In no way was it a very joyful anniversary, for it is lonelier to be lonely on one's birthday than on any other day. Even her little maid
Elizabeth was absent on a visit to her parents, and
Gottlieb, whose own good nature—even if Mr.
Rinkle had not told him to do so—would have

prompted him to come to the house to see if he were needed, had not made his appearance.

"I suppose," thought Mrs. Lent, "that Mr. Rinkle had a good breakfast at Mrs. Sharp's, for she expected him, and it may be—for she is quite forward enough for that sort of thing—that she has persuaded him to take her to the flower show." And here there came a little sigh. "But if he's done that he's done it," she reflected, "and there's no help for it. But I shall put off dinner, and won't have it until he comes home. And then he shall have his mince pie nice and hot as he likes it."

She was turning over the mincemeat with a fork, looking for such pieces of suet as might be large enough to pick out. "Mince pies do not agree with him very well," she said to herself, "but he is very fond of them, and I will take out as much suet as I can and put in a little more brandy. I don't think he will notice it, and it will make it more wholesome."

Her fork now brought up a large raisin, and she held it for a moment, thinking it might be better to cut it in half before putting it back. Mr. Rinkle was very fond of raisins, but to agree with him they ought to be thoroughly cooked. Nicely Lent was a woman who had tender sympathies and pleasant memories, and as she sat with the raisin still on her fork, she thought of other birthdays that had been so different from this. She did not mind on ordinary mornings being left alone in the house, but this morning it was indeed depressing to be there without a soul to speak to her. She could imagine Mr. Rinkle in all the brightness and gladness of the flower show; she could hear the delightful admiration provoked by the Rev. Ezekiel Crump, in whom she felt almost a maternal pride, and she thought with a pang that, perhaps, the Widow Sharp was at that moment making herself officious by dilating to the bystanders upon the merits of this grand pelargonium. And here was she, sitting alone in her kitchen. As she thought thus a large tear trickled down her cheek and dropped upon the raisin.

This aroused her to a sense of the present. It would not do to put a raisin that had been cried on into a pie, and she was about to throw it away. But she hesitated; that tear had been evoked by sweet memories of the past. It seemed like a sacrilege to throw it away. She took the raisin gently from the fork, and going to the window, made a little hole in the mould of a pot of mignonette, which Mr. Rinkle had given her, and buried the raisin therein. It suited her to think that the little rootlets of the mignonette would take up that tear. She put her nose to the delicate blossoms of the plant, and then she returned to her work.

If Mrs. Lent had known that the day before had been Gottlieb Stein's birthday, and that he was now in bed at home, sleeping off the effects of a large supper, which had been given in honour of the anniversary to some chosen friends, she would have hastened to the greenhouses to see if they needed any attention in regard to warmth or ventilation ; and she would have discovered Mr. Rinkle's sorry plight, and her hands would have borne him a ladder.

If Mr. Rinkle had known of Gottlieb's birthday supper and its consequences, he would not so frequently and with such drowsy content have renewed his naps, thinking each time he half opened his eyes that they had been closed but a minute or two, and not imagining that his nature was repaying itself the several hours of sleep of which he had deprived it the night before.

It was nearly noon when, along a path which led from a handsome house upon a hillside half-a-mile away, a young lady appeared walking briskly toward the Rinkle greenhouses. A more charming girl is seldom seen on a bright October morning, or, indeed, upon any other morning.

At this same time there walked along the crest of the hills on the other side of the narrow valley in which the greenhouses lay, a young man with a stick under his arm, who had started out for a long country tramp. But as he turned his head to gaze upon the bright autumnal scenery beneath him, he suddenly stopped.

"Upon my word!" he exclaimed aloud, "I believe that is Clara. Yes, truly it is. She is going down to Nathan Rinkle's greenhouses. What glorious good luck. I wonder if I can get there before her."

There was really no doubt upon this subject, for the young man ran down the hill, vaulted over a fence, crossed a brook, and hurrying through the

Rinkle apple orchard, reached the nearest green-house in a surprisingly short time. He had been there for nearly five minutes, walking up and down, smelling some flowers without perceiving their scent, and looking at others without noticing their colour, when the door opened and the young lady entered. His astute mind had rightly divined that she would go into the house first reached by the path.

With outstretched hand he advanced to meet her, and took no pains to conceal his delight in doing so. She was surprised, and all the prettier for that.

" I have come," she said, as she offered him her hand, " to get this basket filled with flowers. But Mr. Rinkle is not here, I believe."

" No," said the young man. " Shall you wait for him here, or shall we go to look for him ?"

" Oh, I will go to look for him," she said, " but don't let me trouble you, Mr. Hatfield."

" Trouble!" he exclaimed. " As if it were possible." And they went out together.

Young Leonard Hatfield was not the avowed lover of Miss Knightley, but the only reason for

this was that he had never yet had an opportunity
of avowing his passion for her. He had adored
her for what seemed to him a very long time, but
never in her father's mansion on the hill, on the
tennis grounds, or in the houses of friends, had he
found the moment he longed for. Now it seemed
to him that it had come. He would have been
glad to open his heart to her in the quiet greenhouse among the flowers, but she was in such a
hurry to leave it she gave him no time.

The two now entered the next greenhouse, but
they found no one there. Leonard was in favour
of waiting there until someone came, but Clara
would not agree to that; she thought it better to
find someone.

They now went into the principal greenhouse,
and near the door stood a number of plants
covered with beautiful blossoms, and prominent
among these was the Rev. Ezekiel Crump.

Clara was a great lover of flowers. "What
a perfectly beautiful pelargonium this is!" she
exclaimed. "Oh, if I could have one of those
sprays. I wish I could find someone to attend to
me."

"I don't think Mr. Rinkle or any of his men are here," said Leonard, after walking to the other end of the house and calling several times, "but here is someone who can attend to you. Let me cut off this spray and give it to you. I shall be so glad to do it," and he took a knife from his pocket.

"Oh, no, no!" exclaimed Clara, stretching out her hand toward him. "You must not do it. I am sure that is a rare flower, and very likely Mr. Rinkle intends to take it to the flower show at Marston, which opens to-day."

"Oh, no," said Leonard, quite confidently, "he has taken his flowers there long before this. I have no doubt he had a lot of this sort of pelargonium, more than he wanted, and he left this one."

Clara was examining the flower with great interest. "I must find out about this," she said; "I never saw anything like it. Just look at this spray with five great blossoms on it, each of them nearly three inches in diameter! And what exqusite blending of crimson, pink, and green! I wonder what it is called." She stooped and read the name of the plant, which was writtten on a wooden label stuck into the earth of the pot. " How utterly absurd ! " she exclaimed, laughing. " This perfectly beautiful thing is named the Rev. Ezekiel Crump."

She laughed again, and Leonard laughed with her. But he did not intend to waste his time in merriment ; his mind was bent on earnest work. Here was a chance to speak which he must not lose.

" Miss Knightley," he said, " if you will accept from me this new and beautiful flower it will give me a pleasure as new and beautiful as——"

"Oh, you mustn't do it ! " she cried. " Don't touch it, please. I must ask Mr. Rinkle about it, or his man, if he isn't here." And, without further words, she turned and left the greenhouse.

Leonard followed her, disappointed and annoyed. Miss Knightley's abrupt manner showed him that she did not wish to give him an opportunity to speak to her of the new and beautiful pleasure to which he had alluded. But he did not intend to give up the attempt, and he was quickly at her side.

" There is only one other place where they

can be," she said, "they must be in the violet-house."

Leonard did not wish to hurry to the violet-house, or to any other house where they might expect to find people.

"Miss Knightley," said he, "suppose we go there by this broad walk which leads around the gardens. That footpath is very narrow and may be wet."

"Oh, this leads straight to the house," said she, "and that one goes ever so far around." And she immediately took the narrow walk.

When following a lady along a path wide enough for only one, and bordered by tall grass and bushes, it is not often convenient to propose marriage to her, especially if she be walking very fast. But Leonard followed Miss Knightley resolutely. If it were necessary he would walk home with her. This day he would certainly finish what he had begun to say to her.

"I declare," said Miss Knightley, when she had proceeded nearly to the middle of the violet-house, "there is nobody here. I certainly expected to find someone in this place."

"And most happy am I," said Leonard, stepping

R

close to her, "that there is nobody here, for this gives me a chance to tell you, Clara, that I love you ; with all my heart and soul I have long loved you, and I cannot wait any longer to tell you so." In his excitement he took hold of her left hand, her right being occupied with her basket.

Mr. Rinkle wakened when he heard the door of the violet-house open. In an instant he was sitting up alert, and with every sense at its sharpest. " It must be after eight o'clock," he said to himself, " and that rascal has just come. I'll pay him well for this. But I'll wait until he comes nearer, and give him a good fright."

Prepared to give a howl which might come from a wild demon of the depths, Nathan sat leaning forward, and ready to spring to his feet when the miscreant Gottlieb should be near enough. But suddenly his mood changed. " There are the footsteps of two persons," he thought, " and I hear the rustling of a dress. One must be a woman." Then hearing Clara's exclamation, his heart sank. " It's Miss Knightley," he said to himself, " and someone with her. Oh, dear me, I must not let them know I am here! If she should go home and tell her

father she found me down a cistern I'd never hear
the end of it. He'd laugh at me as long as he
lives."

So, crouching down as low as possible, Mr.
Rinkle remained perfectly quiet, hoping that these
untimely visitors might soon leave the house. But
the next moment he heard Leonard's avowal of his
love.

" My conscience ! " thought Nathan, holding his
breath in amazement. " It's that young Hatfield
making love to her. How very embarrassing. Oh
dear ! Oh dear ! It would be awful if they knew
I was so close to them." But in spite of his em-
barrassment, Nathan did not put his fingers to his
ears. His heart had never beat so quickly ; he had
never been more interested.

Leonard continued : " Clara," he said, speaking
earnestly and rapidly, " may I love you ? Can I
hope that you will love me ? Oh ! Do not think
of going away. There is nothing in the world so
important as what I am saying to you."

Clara had looked towards the door, but whether
she contemplated a retreat towards it, or whether
she glanced through its glass panes in the fear that

someone might be approaching, Leonard could not tell; but she saw no one, and it was impossible to retreat, so tightly was her hand held. She turned her head from the door, and bent her eyes upon the ground.

"Oh, Clara!" he exclaimed, "will you not speak to me? Will you not look at me?"

She did not speak, but she looked up at him. That was enough.

"How very embarrassing," thought Mr. Rinkle, his ears expanding like opening calla lilies, and his heart beating faster in his excited interest. "She must have agreed, for they surely are kissin'. Yes, I can hear them, and most likely hugging. Mercy on me! It's lucky they don't know I'm here. How dreadful it would be if they even heard me breathe!" And as this thought came to him he pressed his lips closely together.

"Oh, happy, happy day!" cried Leonard. "Oh, glorious world! Oh, darling Clara—my own for ever."

"Dear me, dear me!" thought Mr. Rinkle, "how warmed up he is. And I don't wonder. I wonder if he really is holding her in his arms. Yes, he must be. That was another kiss."

Some calla lilies are so large that it was impossible for Mr. Rinkle's ears to rival their dimensions, but they did their best.

"And you really are mine—for ever and always?" asked the ardent lover.

And into the violet-perfumed air of the greenhouse there was breathed the one word "Yes."

"There," thought Mr. Rinkle, "that is the first thing she has said. But, to be sure, he hasn't given her a chance. What! Again and again! I almost wish they would go away. This is getting to be very embarrassing."

"Come, darling," said Leonard, "let us go. And nothing shall now prevent my giving that loveliest flower to the loveliest woman on earth. It shall be my first present to her, and a fit one. She shall carry home, my love, and with it the finest spray of blossom from the Rev. Ezekiel Crump."

"Don't you do it!" screamed Mr. Rinkle, springing to his feet. "Don't you touch it! I'm going to take that flower to the show. I wouldn't have it spoiled for the world."

There was a scream from Clara; a shout from Leonard. Then the young lady began to tremble and sat down on the floor. Her lover assisted her to

lean back against one of the supports of the violet
beds, and then, seeing that she had not really
fainted, he sprang to the open mouth of the cistern.
There, a little below the surface of the floor, he saw
the pale face of Mr. Rinkle, who was standing on
the bucket.

"I beg a thousand pardons, Mr. Hatfield," said
the trembling florist, dismayed at what he had
done, "and I vow I wouldn't have heard a word of
what you were saying if it had been possible for
me to sink any deeper into the bowels of the earth.
There is a ladder at the far end of the greenhouse,
and if you will put that down here, Mr. Hatfield,
I'll come up and tell you all about it."

Leonard was so amazed, so shocked, and so
angry, that he could find no words in which to
reply to this apparition in the cistern, but he
brought the ladder, and very soon the florist was
standing before him and Clara, who had now risen
to her feet.

"This is very embarrassing," said the florist, his
hands clasped before him.

"Now then," said Leonard, fiercely, "none of
that nonsense. I got you out to hear what you had

to say about this contemptible piece of business."

Mr. Rinkle looked first at the angry young man
and then at the pale Clara, and told everything just
as it happened. " You see," said he in conclusion,
" I kept so very quiet thinking to frighten Gottlieb,
that you two began speakin' in a way that might
be called confidential before I had time to let you
know that there was someone else in the greenhouse ; and then I didn't like to speak out because
I knew it would embarrass you so dreadfully, and
I felt at any moment you might be on the p'int of
going away. As for me, I assure you I never was
more embarrassed since the beginning of my days."

" Look here," said Leonard, " I want to know if
you heard everything we said ? "

" Oh, no, indeed," replied the good Nathan.
" There were times when I couldn't hear a word.
You see I was at the very bottom of the cistern.
But of course I couldn't help understandin' the
drift of the conversation, which seemed in a way
to betoken that you two were engaged to be
married."

Miss Knightley, whose colour had come back to

her face, looked at Leonard ; he looked at her, and they both laughed. Mr. Rinkle saw his opportunity and extended a hand to each. "Let me congratulate you," said he, "and I beg from the bottom of my heart that you won't mind an old fellow like me gettin' by the merest accident a hint of your engagement before anybody else. And you may trust me for never sayin' a word to a livin' soul about it ; as far as that goes it might have been one of them pots that was down in the cistern."

There was a moment of silence, and Clara was the first to speak.

"It is dreadfully embarrassing, as you say, Mr. Rinkle, but it can't be helped now, and I am willing to forgive you. But you must promise not only not to mention our engagement until we are ready to announce it, but that you will never, never to the end of your days, mention to a living soul that you were anywhere near at the time it was made."

"Oh, bless me!" cried Mr. Rinkle, "I'll never do that. It would make me the laughing-stock of the country."

"If I ever hear," said Leonard, "that this has leaked out, I shall make it my business that the people in this neighbourhood shall never go to one of your greenhouses without sending somebody ahead to see who is in the cistern."

"Oh, you need have no fear of that," said Nathan, "and now you must excuse me for leaving you so abruptly. I must hurry off to the flower show. I haven't my watch with me, but it must be a good deal after eight o'clock."

"After eight!" exclaimed Leonard, taking out his watch, "it is half-past twelve."

Mr. Rinkle stood aghast. "I must have slept the whole morning," he said, woefully. "And that settles me at the flower show. The prizes were to be given out at noon to-day, while things are fresh, and there is no use in my thinking of going there at this time. It is all up with me and my exhibition, at least the best part of it."

An idea suddenly struck the florist. "Stay here, please," he said, "I'll be back in a minute." And he ran out of the house.

In a short time he returned, bearing in his hand the largest spray of blossoms from the Rev.

Ezekiel Crump. "It's no use letting them stay until they are withered," he said, "and as the plant can't enter for a prize now I'll let you, Mr. Hatfield, do what you wanted to do, and give your lady a flower that no other lady ever had before. If you knew how I worked and waited to get those blossoms you'd know the value of them."

This extinguished the last spark of resentment in Leonard's mind, and Mr. Rinkle considerately absented himself during the presentation of the flowers.

It was evening; dinner was over, and Mr. Rinkle pushed back his chair with an air of great content. At the hasty luncheon, which he ate standing and in a perturbation of mind, quite natural after what had happened, he had merely stated to Mrs. Lent that he had not gone to the flower show because Gottlieb had not come to take charge. But now, during dinner, he had given Mrs. Lent a full account of his misadventures, alluding to his rescue from the cistern only by saying that Mr. Hatfield had happened to come into the violet-house and had helped him out.

"That was a wonderfully good mince pie, Mrs.

Lent," he remarked in his after-dinner serenity, "there never was a better."

" If I had only known," said Mrs. Lent, "that while I was making it you were down in that dreadful hole, how fast I would have run to you."

Mr. Rinkle crossed his legs and smiled. He was in a state of great good humour. " I know you would, Mrs. Lent, I know you would. But, after all, perhaps it is just as well you didn't come."

She looked surprised. " Don't you think I could have helped you out as well as anybody ? "

" Of course you could. I wasn't thinking of that," said Nathan, walking up and down the floor and still smiling. Suddenly he struck his hands together, and then he took his hat from its peg. " Mrs. Lent," said he, " don't clear away the dinner things. I'll be back in a minute."

When he returned he brought with him the second largest spray of flowers from the Rev. Ezekiel Crump, bearing four great blossoms.

" Nicely," said he, " allow me to present to the loveliest woman on earth the loveliest flower, at least of the pelargonium family, that was ever grown by man."

Mrs. Lent stood up amazed. Never before had he called her Nicely; and what did he mean by bringing her that almost sacred flower? "I don't understand," she gasped.

"Nicely, said he, "may I love you? Will you love me in return? Come now, don't look down or think about doing kitchen work. There is nothing so important as what I am saying to you."

She understood now. Flushing and trembling, she could not speak, but she looked up at him, and that was enough. As for Nathan, he forgot nothing of the lesson he had learned.

It was an hour afterward. The room was in order and the two were sitting by the fire. He had just finished giving her a full account of the interview he had overheard between Miss Knightley and Mr. Hatfield. "Of course, I wouldn't have told you," he said, "so long as we were merely good friends, but now that we are the same as one, I couldn't help tellin' you. It's your right to know all I know."

The widow was so well aware of Nathan's desire to tell things about people that a faint suspicion came into her mind that perhaps he had proposed to her because there was no other way in which he could justify himself in telling her this wonderful bit of news. But she dismissed the thought as an unworthy one.

"After all," exclaimed the jubilant Nathan, "the Rev. Ezekiel Crump brought me a prize. He brought me you."

Mrs. Lent looked at him inquiringly. "What had he to do with it?" she said.

He turned a beaming face toward her, "Nicely," said he, "if them two had gone away without knowing I was in the cistern, and I'd had to wait until Gottlieb came and got me out, and that rascal didn't show himself until two o'clock this afternoon, there'd been a fight; and as he is a big fellow, and I'd been a fiery mad one, I wouldn't have been in a fit state this day to make love to anyone. But it was the name of the Rev. Ezekiel Crump that brought me bouncing to my feet and got me out of that hole, while I was in such a state of mind hearin' what I heard and thinkin' about what I imagined, that I was one tingle of glowin' excitement from my head that was in the air to my feet that were in the water, and I kept thinkin' and thinkin' about it, till early in the afternoon I made up my mind that as soon as I could get the day's work done and dinner was over, I wouldn't wait any longer to declare my love, just as young Hatfield couldn't wait any longer to declare his."

"Nathan," said she, "did hearing those two put this disposition into you?"

He threw one arm over the back of her chair. "No, indeed, Nicely," said he, "it only brought it out."

The next day Mr. Rinkle went to the flower show dressed in his best clothes and wearing in his button-hole the remaining spray of blossoms from his new pelargonium. His brother florists stared with amazement at his adornment. "If you had brought yesterday the plant that bore that flower," one of them exclaimed, "you would have gained a first prize."

"Oh, I got prize enough," said Nathan, with an air of superiority to floricultural distinctions, "and the Rev. Ezekiel Crump must wait until next year for his turn."

GRANDISON'S QUANDARY.

GRANDISON PRATT was a coloured man of about thirty, who, with his wife and two or three children, lived in a neat log cabin in one of the Southern States of America. He was a man of a very independent turn of mind, and he much desired to own the house in which he lived and the small garden patch around it. This valuable piece of property belonged to Mr. Morris, and as it was an outlying corner of his large farm he had no objection to sell it to Grandison, provided the latter could pay for it; but of this he had great doubts. The man was industrious enough, but he often seemed to have a great deal of difficulty about paying the very small rental charged for his place, and Mr. Morris, consequently, had well-grounded doubts about his ability to purchase it.

"But, sah," said Grandison one day, when these

objections had been placed before him, " I's been turning dis thing ober in my min' ober and ober. I know jes' how much I kin make an' how much I's got to spend an' how I kin save ter buy the house, and if I agree to pay you so much money on such a day an' so much on such anudder day I'se gwine ter do it. You kin jes' put that down, sah, for sartin shuh."

"Well, Grandison," said Mr. Morris, " I'll give you a trial. If at the end of six months you can pay me the first instalment, I'll have the necessary papers made out, and you can go on and buy the place; but if you are not up to time on the first payment, I want to hear no more about the purchase."

" All right, Mahs'r Morris," said Grandison. " If I gibs you my word ter pay de money on de fus' day ob October, I's gwine to do it. Dat's sartin shuh."

Months passed on, and, although Grandison worked as steadily as usual, he found towards the end of September that, in the ordinary course of things, he would never be able to make up the sum necessary for the first payment. Other methods out of the ordinary course came into his mind, but he had doubts about availing himself of them. He was extremely anxious to make up the amount due, for he knew very well that if he did not pay it on the day appointed he might bid farewell to his hope of becoming a freeholder. In his perplexity he resolved to consult Brother 'Bijah, the minister of the little church in the pine woods, to which Grandison belonged.

"Now, look-a-heah, Brudder 'Bijah," said he, "wot's I gwine to do 'bout dis bizness. I done promised ter pay dis money on de fus' day ob de comin' month, an' dar's $6 ob it dat I ain't got yit."

"An' ain't der any way ter git it?" asked 'Bijah.

"Yaas, dar's one way," said Grandison. "I's been turnin' dis matter ober an' ober in my min', an' dar's only one way. I mought sell apples. Apples is mighty skarse dis fall, an' I kin git $2 a bar'l for 'em in town. Now, if I was ter sell three bar'ls of apples I'd hab dat $6 sartin shuh. Don' you see dat, Brudder 'Bijah?"

"Dat's all clar 'nuff," said the minister, "but whar you gwine ter get three bar'ls o' apples?

S

You don't mean ter tell me dat you's got 'nuf apple trees in your little gyardin fur ter shake down three bar'ls o' apples."

" Now, look a-heah, Brudder 'Bijah," said Grandison, his eyes sparkling with righteous indignation, "dat's too much to 'spec' of a man who's got ter work all day to s'port his wife and chillun. I digs, an' ploughs, an' I plants, an' I hoes, an' if anybody gibes me any gwahner I dusts dat on de groun'. But all dem things ain't 'nuf ter make apple trees grow in my gyardin like as dey was cohnfiel' peas."

" Dat's so," said 'Bijah, reflectively. " Dat's too much to 'spec' ob any man. But how's you gwine ter sell de apples if you ain't got 'em ? "

" I's got ter git 'em," said Grandison. " Dar's apples 'nuff growin' roun', an' not so fur away dat I can't tote 'em ter my house in a basket. It's powerful hard on a man wot's worked all day ter have ter tote apples ahfter night, but dar ain't no other way ob gittin' dat dar money."

" I 'spec' de orchard whar you's thinkin' o' gwine is Mahs'r Morrises," said the minister.

" You don' 'spose I'se gwine ter any ob dose low

down orchards on de udder side de crick, does ye?
Mahs'r Morris has got de bes' apples in dis county.
Dat's de kin' wot fotch $2 a bar'l."

"Brudder Gran'son," said 'Bijah, solemnly, "is
you min' runnin' on takin' Mahs'r Morrises apples
inter town an' sellin' 'em?"

"Well, he gits de money, don't he?" answered
the other, "and if I don't sell his apples, 'tain't no
use sellin' none. Dem udder little nubbins roun'
heah won't fetch no $2 a bar'l."

"Dem ain't justifyin' deeds wot's runnin' in your
mind," said 'Bijah. "Dey ain't justifyin'."

"Ob course," said Grandison, "dey wouldn't be
justifyin' if I had de six dollars. But I ain't got
'em, an' I'se promised to pay 'em. Now, is I ter
stick to de truf, or isn't I?"

"Truf is mighty," said the preacher, "an' ought
not to be hendered from prevailin'."

"Dat's so! dat's so!" exclaimed Grandison.
"You can't go agin de Scripters. Truf *is* mighty,
an't 'taint fur pore human critters like us to try to
upsot her. Wot we're got ter do is ter stick to her
through thick an' thin'."

"Ob course, dat's wot we oughter do," said

S 2

'Bijah, " but I can't see my way clar to you sellin' dem apples."

" But dar ain't nuffin else ter do ! " exclaimed Grandison, "an' ef I don't do dat, away goes de truf, clar out o' sight.   An' wot sort of 'ligion you call dat, Brudder 'Bijah ? "

"'Taint no kind at all," said 'Bijah, " fur we's bound ter stick to de truf, which is de bottom corner-stone ob piousness.   But dem apples don't seem ter git demselves straightened out in my mind, Brudder Gran'son."

" It 'pears ter me, Brudder 'Bijah, dat you doan' look at dem apples in de right light.   If I was gwine to sell 'em to git money ter buy a lot o' spotted calliker to make frocks fur de chillen, or eben ter buy two pars o' shoes fur me an' Judy ter go to church in, dat would be a sin sartin shuh. But you done furgit dat I's gwine ter take de money straight off ter Mahs'r Morris.   If apples is riz and I gets $2.25 a bar'l, ob course I keeps de extry quarter, which don' pay anyhow fur de trouble ob pickin' and haulin' em.   But de $6 I gibs, cash down, ter Mahs'r Morris.   Don' you call dat puffectly fa'r an' squar', Brudder 'Bijah ? "

'Bijah shook his head. "Dis a mighty dubersome question, Brudder Gran'son, a mighty dubersome question."

Grandison stood with a disappointed expression
on his countenance. He greatly desired to gain
from his minister sanction for the financial operation he had proposed. But this the solemn 'Bijah
did not appear prepared to give. As the two men
stood together by the roadside they saw, riding
toward them, Mr. Morris himself.

"Now den," exclaimed Grandison, "heah comes
Mahs'r Morris, and I's gwine ter put dis question
to hisse'f. He oughter know how ter 'cide 'bout it
if anybody does."

"You ain't gwine ter tell him 'bout dem apples,
is ye?" asked 'Bijah, quickly.

"No, sah," replied the other. "I's gwine to put
the case on a diff'rent show-pint. But 'twill be the
same thing as de udder."

Mr. Morris was a genial-natured man, who took
a great deal of interest in his negro neighbours,
and was fond of listening to their peculiar humour.
Therefore, when he saw that Grandison wished to
speak to him he readily pulled up his horse.

"Mahs'r Morris," said Grandison, removing his hat, "Brudder 'Bijah an' me has been argyin' on de subjick ob truf. An' jes' as you was comin' up I was gwine ter tell him a par'ble, 'bout sticken ter truf. An' if you's got time, Mahs'r Morris, I'd be pow'ful glad ter tell you de par'ble, and let you 'cide 'tween us."

"Very well," said Mr. Morris, settling himself easily in his saddle, "go on with your parable."

II.

"Dis yere par'ble," said Grandison, "has got a justifyin' meanin' in it, an' it's 'bout a b'ar an' a possum. De 'possum, he was a-gwine out early in de mawnin' ter git a little cohn fur his break-fus'—"

"Very wrong in the opossum," said Mr. Morris, "for I am sure he hadn't planted any corn."

"Well, den, sah," said Grandison, "p'raps 'twas akerns! but, anyway, afore he was out ob de woods he see a big ole b'ar a-comin' straight 'long to him. De 'possum he ain't got no time ter climb a tree an' git out on de leetlest end ob a long limb, an' so he lay hese'f flat down on de groun' an' make b'lieve he's dead. When de ole bar came up he sot down an' look at de 'possum. Fus' he turn his head on one side, an' den he turn his head on de udder, but he look at de 'possum all de time. D'rectly he gits done lookin', an' he says :

" ' Look-a-head, 'possum, is you dead or is you libin' ? If you's dead I won't eat you, fur I neber eat dead critters, but if you's libin' den I eat you for breakfus', fur I is bilin' hungry, not havin' had nuffin sence sun-up but a little snack dat I took afore gwine out into the damp air ob de mawnin'. Now, den, 'possum, speak out an' tell me, is you 'libe or is you dead ? '

" Dat are question frew de 'possum inter a pow'ful sweat. If he tole de truf an' said he was alibe he knowed well 'nuf dat de bar would gobble him up quicker'n if he'd been a hot ash cake an' a bowl of buttermilk ; but if he said he was dead so's de bar wouldn't eat him, de bar, like 'nuf, would know he lied, an' would eat him all de same. So he turned de matter ober in his min', an' he wrastled wid his 'victions, but he couldn't come ter no 'clusion. ' Now don't you tink,' said de bar, ' dat I's got time to sit here de whole mawnin' waitin' fer you ter make up your mind whether you's dead or not.   If you don't 'cide pretty quick I'll put a big rock a-top o' you, an' stop fer your answer when I come back in de ebenin'.'   Now dis gib de 'possum a pow'ful skeer, an' 'twas cl'ar to his min' dat he mus' 'cide de question straight off.   If he tole de truf, and said he was alibe, he'd be eat up shuh ; but if he said he was dead, de bar mought b'lieve him.   'Twarnt very likely dat he would, but dar was one leetle chance, an' he done took it.   ' I is dead,' says he. ' You's a long time makin' up your min' 'bout it,' says de bar.   ' How long you been dead ?'   ' Sence day 'fore yestidday,' say the 'possum.   ' All right !' says de bar, ' when dey've on'y been dead two or free days, an' kin talk, I eats 'em all de same.' An' he eat him up."

"And now, Grandison," said Mr. Morris, " where is the moral of that parable ? "

"De moral is dis," said Grandison ; " stick ter de truf.   If de 'possum had tole de truf, an' said he was alibe, de bar couldn't eat him no more'n he did eat him ; no bar could do dat.   An' I axes you, Mahs'r Morris, don' dat par'ble show dat eb'rybody oughter stick ter de truf, no matter what happens."

"Well, I don't think your moral is very clear," said Mr. Morris, "for it would have been about as bad for the 'possum one way as the other. But, after all, I suppose it would have been better for the little beast to tell the truth and die with a clear conscience."

"Dat's so!" cried Brother 'Bijah, speaking in his ministerial capacity, "de great thing in dis worl' is ter die wid a clear conscience."

"But you can't do dat," said Grandison, "if you let dis thing an' dat thing come in ter hinder ye. Now dat's jes' wot we's been disputin' 'bout, Mahs'r Morris. I 'clared dat we oughter stick ter de truf widout lookin' to de right or de lef'; but Brudder 'Bijah, his min' wasn't quite made up on de subjick. Now, wot you say, Mahs'r Morris?"

"I say stick to the truth, of course," said Mr. Morris, gathering up his reins. "And, by the way, Grandison, do you expect to make that payment on your place, which is due next week?"

"Yaas, sah, sartin shuh," said Grandison. "I done tole you I'd do it, Mahs'r Morris, an' I 'tends ter stick ter de truf."

"Now, den," said Grandison, in a tone of triumph, when Mr. Morris had ridden away, "you see J's right in my 'clusions, and Mahs'r Morris 'grees with me."

"Dunno," said Brother 'Bijah, shaking his head, "dis is a mighty dubersome question. You kep' dem apples clar out o' sight, Brudder Gran'son; clar out o' sight."

It was about a week after this, quite early in the morning, that Grandison was slowly driving into town with a horse and a waggon which he had borrowed from a neighbour. In the waggon were three barrels of fine apples. Suddenly, at a turn in the road, he was greatly surprised to meet Mr. Morris, riding homeward.

"What have you in those barrels, Grandison?" inquired his landlord.

"Dey's apples, sah," was the reply, "dat I's got de job ob haulin' ter town, sah."

Mr. Morris rode up to the waggon and removed the piece of old canvas that was thrown over the tops of the barrels. There was no need of asking any questions. No one but himself, for many

miles around, had " Bellflowers " and " Jeannettes "
like these.

" How much do you lack, Grandison," he said,
"of making up the money you owe me to-
morrow ? "

" Six dollars, sah," said Grandison.

" Six dollars—three barrels—very good," said
Mr. Morris. " I see you are determined to stick
to the truth, Grandison, and keep your engagement. But I will trouble you to turn that waggon
round and haul those apples home. And, if you
still want to buy the place, you can come on
Monday morning and work out the balance you
have to make up on the first instalment ; and,
after this, you can make all your payments in
work. A day's labour is fair and plain, but I
can't expect to see through your ways of getting
money."

It was not long after this that Grandison was
ploughing in one of Mr. Morris's fields, when Brother
'Bijah came along and sat upon the fence.

" Gran'son," said he, when the ploughman had
reached the end of the furrow, and was preparing

to turn, " jes' you let your hoss res' a minnit till I tell you a par'ble."

" Wot par'ble ? " said Grandison in a tone of unconcern, but stopping his horse all the same.

" Why dis one ! " said 'Bijah.   " Dar was an ole mule an' he b'longed to a cullud man named Harris, who used ter carry de mail from de Coht House ter Cary's cross-roads.   De ole mule was a pow'ful triflin' critter an' he got lazier an' lazier, an 'ore long he got so dreffle slow dat it tuk him more'n one day ter go from de Coht House ter de cross-roads, an' he allus come in de day ahfter mail-day, when de people was done gone home. So de cullud man, Harris, he says :

" ' You is too ole fur ter carry de mail, you triflin' mule, an' I hain't got no udder use fur you.'

" So he put him in a gully-fiel', whar dar was nuffin but bar' groun' an' hog weed.   Now, dar was nuffin in dis worl' dat triflin' mule hated so much as hog weed, and he says to hese'f : ' I's boun' ter do somefin' better'n dis fur a libin.   I reckin I'll go skeer dat ole Harris, an' make him gib me a feed o' meal.'   So he jump ober de fence, fur he was spry 'nuf when he had a min' ter, an' he steals an ole bar skin dat he'd seen hangin' up in de stoh po'ch an' he pretty nigh kivered himse'f all up wid it. Den he go down to de pos' offis, whar de mail had jes' cum in. When dis triflin' ole mule seed de cullud man, Harris, sittin' on de bottom step ob de po'ch, he begin to kick up his heels an' make all de noise he could wid his mouf. 'Wot's dat?' cried de cullud man, Harris. 'I's a big grizzly bar,' said de mule, ''scaped from de 'nagerie when 'twas fordin' Scott's Crick.' 'When did you git out?' said de cullud man, Harris. 'I bus' from de cage at half-pas' free o'clock dis ebenin'.' 'An' is you reelly a grizzly bar?' 'Dat's de truf,' said the triflin' mule, 'an' I's pow'ful hungry, an' if you don' go git me a feed o' meal I'll swaller you down whole.' An' he begun to roar as like a grizzly bar as he knew how. 'Dat all de truf, you tellin' me?' de cullud man, Harris, ask. 'Dat's all true as I's libin',' says de triflin' mule. 'All right den,' says de cullud man, Harris, "if you kin come from de ford on Scott's Crick in a hour an' a half, you kin carry de mail jes' as well as any udder mule, an' I's gwine ter buy a big cart whip, an' make you do it. So take off dat bar skin, an' come 'long wid

me.' "So you see, Brudder Gran'son," continued
'Bijah, "dar's dif'rent kinds of truf, an' you's got
ter be mighty 'ticklar wot kind you sticks ter."

"Git up," said Grandison to his drowsy horse, as
he started him on another furrow.

www.ingramcontent.com/pod-product-compliance
Lightning Source LLC
Chambersburg PA
CBHW020340030726
47496CB00007B/1956